"The great storm
is coming. . . ."

Curse of the Ancients

INFINITY RING

Curse of the Ancients

Matt de la Peña

Walla Walla
County Libraries

SCHOLASTIC INC.

For teachers everywhere, especially my two favorites:
Al and Roni de la Peña
—M.d.l.P.

Library of Congress Cataloging-in-Publication Data available

ISBN 978-0-545-38699-9
10 9 8 7 6 5 4 3 2 1   13 14 15 16 17

Cover illustration by Chris Nurse and Cheung Tai
Book and cover design by Keirsten Geise
Back cover photography of characters by Michael Frost © Scholastic Inc.

First edition, June 2013
Printed in China   62

Scholastic US: 557 Broadway · New York, NY 10012
Scholastic Canada: 604 King Street West · Toronto, ON M5V 1E1
Scholastic New Zealand Limited: Private Bag 94407 · Greenmount, Manukau 2141
Scholastic UK Ltd.: Euston House · 24 Eversholt Street · London NW1 1DB

PROLOGUE

EVERY OTHER time Sera has warped through history with Dak and Riq, it's happened in an instant. She gets sucked into a void, her stomach climbing up into her throat, her whole body shifting into floating particles, no longer a solid thing—it's beyond any roller-coaster free fall imaginable. And then, just before she gets sick, she opens her eyes in another time and place.

But this warp is not like the others.

Instead of time speeding up, it slows down.

And a wall lifts inside her mind.

She sees herself hurrying through flooding streets, out of breath, underneath a blistering twilight sky. Thick tornados ripping through neighborhoods in the distance. The bloodred sun hovering closer to Earth than seems possible, electrical surges shooting out from its core, making the swirling wind intolerably hot and sticky. Acid rain gushing down in slanted sheets. People leaning out of upper-story windows. All of them wide-eyed and screaming. Holding one another.

But Sera can't afford to stop and help.

She has to keep moving. Has to get where she's going before it's too late.

She is alone now, but she didn't come here alone. Ilsa was with her. Ilsa, her enemy. Sera left her behind where she had collapsed, left her with a promise to return. A promise to get them both to safety.

But not yet. Sera has something to do first.

The water rushing through the streets rises quickly until it's nearly head high, and Sera is forced to scale a fire escape where she shoves up against a wall, sucking in breaths and looking all around her. The world is ending. Right before her eyes.

She spots a small motorized emergency raft tied to a looted fire truck. No one inside. She launches herself toward it, splashing into the water and swimming frantically. She hacks the rope in half with a switchblade, climbs in, and hot-wires the engine. In seconds she's speeding through intersection after intersection, steering herself around all the bodies floating facedown in the water. Some are children. Some, old people. She moves past men who squat alone on overturned cars, expressionless as zombies.

One man turns and looks Sera dead in the face as she veers around him, sending a chill down her spine. Because, in his lifeless eyes, she sees the truth of the Cataclysm.

It's not only the disintegration of the world, but the world's people, too.

That's when Sera realizes she's screaming. She's screaming and crying and gunning the raft, shouting at anyone within earshot, "Somebody help us! This can't be happening!"

But it is.

All around her, there are military trucks on their sides and old stubborn trees split down the middle and charred black, people flushed from their homes by the surging floods. Gaps are opening up in the Earth's crust, splitting roads in half, swallowing entire buildings, clusters of people reaching out for help, calling the names of loved ones who are no longer alive.

Sera zips past all of it, turning onto her childhood street.

She lets off the gas as she nears her house, then dives overboard and swim-walks her way up the flooded driveway, fearing the unspeakable horrors she's afraid she'll find inside, what will she find inside, what will she find . . .

Just as she reaches a trembling hand out for the doorknob, though, the memory slips away.

Storm Warnings

SERA OPENED her eyes, shaking.

She was kneeling in clay-colored dirt, completely out of breath and clutching the Infinity Ring to her chest. The first thing she saw when she looked up was a short, dark-skinned woman dressed in a tunic-like *huipil*, holding a baby in each arm, hurrying past what looked to be some kind of ancient temple. A boy and a girl, both younger than Sera, ran by next, followed by a man wearing an elaborate headdress.

Sera turned to Dak and Riq. They were watching the same thing: dozens of people rushing past them, trying to get away from something.

But what?

Sera's heart still pounded inside her chest.

These trips through time were typically hard enough on her body, but this one had been different. It seemed to have shaken loose part of her repressed memory of the Cataclysm. During a previous mission, she'd taken an accidental trip to the future, which had given her a glimpse of the end of the world. When Sera came back, though, she was so traumatized by the experience she could only remember a few details, as if unconsciously protecting herself from what she knew she couldn't handle. So, technically, it hadn't been a lie when she told Dak and Riq she had nothing of interest to tell them about her warp without them.

Now that she remembered reaching for her door, though, she was desperate to recall what she had found inside her house. Why couldn't she remember?

Sera shook the Cataclysm from her mind for now and forced herself to take in her surroundings. The three of them were partially hidden behind a row of trees. The sky was full of clouds. The air smelled clean, the way it sometimes did just before rain.

"Dude, why are you crying?"

Sera turned and found Dak staring at her. "I'm not crying," she said, straightening her posture. "Why would I be crying?"

"Uh, I don't know," he said. "That's kind of why I asked."

Sera dismissed him with the wave of a hand and stood up, reaching for her face on the sly — sure enough, warm tears met the tips of her fingers. "I'm definitely not crying!" she snapped at her supposed best friend. "Maybe the time travel's just getting harder on our bodies. Did you ever think about *that*, Dak?"

"It's definitely getting harder on mine," Riq said. He gave Sera a subtle nod that meant he had her back.

Dak stood up, too. "What time period are we in anyway? There are supposed to be Spanish conquistadores all over this place, right? And Franciscan monks. The Yucatán was crawling with those guys in 1562. All I see are scared-looking Mayas."

Sera studied the people hurrying past the temple across from them. It was true, they were all Mayan. She looked down at the Infinity Ring. They were supposed to have landed in 1562. She was sure she'd programmed in the right coordinates.

"Who has the SQuare?" Riq asked.

Sera handed it to him, saying, "According to the display, we're in Izamal. I don't understand what I could've done wrong."

She watched Riq study the screen, then step out from behind the trees to stop a passing boy. "Friend, please hold on for a second," he said in a foreign popping tongue that Sera's translation device had momentary trouble rendering into English. "Where is everyone going?"

The boy slowed. After looking the three time travelers up and down, he shouted, "The great storm is coming! Everyone must find shelter right away!"

The boy turned and hurried off.

Sera looked up along with Dak and Riq. The sky was full of gray clouds, sure, but it didn't look like anything out of the ordinary. Definitely not a "great storm." Then again, according to what she'd learned in school, the Maya were incredibly superstitious. Maybe something had gone wrong at one of their ceremonies.

Dak must've been thinking the same thing because he kept shaking his head. "Funny, I thought we would be the ones running for our lives." He turned to Riq and Sera, clearly readying himself for one of his infamous historical rants. "You *do* know that the Maya are considered a violent and hedonistic civilization, right? They sacrificed people, and they were always at war, and they ate the hearts of their own dead family members."

"Never read about any heart eating," Riq said.

"Okay, maybe not that last part, but   "

"That's enough, Dak," Sera said.

"What? Their big contribution to the world was that they wrote the Great Mayan Codex. And it's only considered great because it warned us of the curse, how our world is heading toward a massive Cataclysm—"

"And that our only hope was a group that would one day come along known as the SQ," Riq interrupted. "We've all read the same history books, Dak."

Sera cringed at the mention of the Cataclysm. She pictured herself reaching for the door of her house again. And then nothing. *Concentrate on the here and now,* she told herself, taking the SQuare back from Riq and rechecking their last series of instructions. They seemed straightforward enough. "Help the Maya. 1562." Then a series of coordinates for the Ring.

Dak tapped Sera on the arm and motioned toward Riq. "I liked it better when we hated this guy."

"We never hated him," Sera said.

"Speak for yourself."

"Believe me," Riq said. "The feeling was mutual."

"Maybe we should turn back the clock," Dak said. He elbowed Sera and gave her a big, goofy smile. "Get it? Turn back the clock?" He pointed at the Infinity Ring tucked safely back inside the satchel hanging from her belt.

"You truly are a child," Riq said.

"And you're a clown."

"Stop," Sera said. "Please. I need to think. If there are no conquistadores, like Dak said, maybe we really are in the wrong time. Because we're definitely in the correct geographical area."

"You really don't think we're in 1562?" Riq said.

"I don't." Sera looked back down at the SQuare. There had to be some scientific explanation for this. Science had never failed her before.

"There's no way we're in 1562," Dak said. "All you have to do is look at that temple across the way. If it was 1562, it would have already been turned into a church. The first thing the Franciscans did when they arrived from Spain was modify the major temples into churches. They wanted to teach the locals there were other ways to live. I can't believe you guys don't know that!"

"Easy, Dak," Sera said. "I'm not feeling real patient right now."

Just then, the sky exploded in thunder directly above them.

A light rain began to fall.

Sera looked up, shielding her eyes with her free hand. The clouds seemed darker now. And the wind was beginning to stir. The Mayas continued hurrying past them along the sparkling white road into the distance.

"Take shelter!" a man shouted. "The great storm is coming."

What "great storm"? Sera thought. And what did these people know about predicting the weather anyway? Back home, meteorologists only got it right about a third of the time, and they had the most up-to-date equipment known to man.

"Come on," Riq said. "Let's go find a place out of the rain. And we have to do something about these Japanese clothes."

"It was fun being a samurai while it lasted," Dak said sadly.

As they stepped out from behind the trees and started across the raised white road, Dak poked Sera in the shoulder. "It really did look like you were crying. Was it because the Ring took us to the wrong time?"

Sera shook her head and focused her eyes in front of her. She was done thinking about the Cataclysm. They had too much work to do.

"Did you have one of those Remnant things?"

"I wasn't crying, Dak!" Sera snapped. "Just leave it alone already."

"Jeez," Dak said. "Bite my head off. Maybe I just wanted to make sure you were okay."

The sky lit up with lightning, followed by the crashing sound of more thunder. All three of them cowered as they ran.

Sera followed Dak and Riq behind a short row of stone huts, her mind slipping back to the horrible details of what she'd seen and heard of the Cataclysm. The sounds of screams over a chorus of never-ending sirens. The earth's violent shifting under her feet every few minutes.

They had to fix the rest of the Breaks or else.

And warping to the wrong time wasn't exactly a promising start.

Fashionably Early

WHEN DAK saw Sera emerge from behind the sculpture-covered stone wall, he had to cover his mouth with a fist to stifle a laugh.

"What?" Sera said.

"Nothing," Dak told her, launching into a fit of fake coughing.

She was dressed in a crazy-looking sack with a hole cut out for her head, as well as a long, colorful skirt that dragged in the dirt behind her when she walked. But the weirdest part was how closely she resembled one of them. The Mayas. Same skin color and high cheekbones. Same coarse, dark hair. If Sera wanted, she could probably pass for a local.

Now was not the time to bring it up, of course. They'd just downloaded a seemingly impossible riddle on the SQuare. And Dak had been best friends with Sera long enough to know when not to mess with her.

"Go on, Dak," Sera said.

"I promise," he told her. "It's nothing."

"Say it!" she demanded.

The look on her face told him she wasn't going to drop it. "Okay, fine," he said. "I was just thinking about . . . um, how nice of an outfit that is."

"Like your loincloth is any better?" Sera said, pointing below his waist.

"It's not a loincloth," Dak said, instinctively covering himself. "It's a breechcloth." He looked down at the clothes Riq had swiped for him off of a tree near a cluster of empty huts. "And maybe your vision's been compromised from all that crying you were doing back there, but I'm also clearly wearing pants —"

"More like leggings," Sera said.

Dak turned to Riq for help. He was wearing the exact same outfit. But Riq was too busy peeking out from under the overhang that was keeping them out of the rain, watching the Mayas continuing to hurry past.

Dak sighed.

Sometimes it got lonely trying to rescue history all by himself.

"Can I see the riddle one more time?" Riq asked, turning back to the others.

Sera handed over the SQuare, and the three of them studied the nonsensical words for the tenth time:

A snake charmer and a clown
A treasure that never was

*A gift from the deity Itzamna: from 9.10.5.10.7 to
   11.17.2.13.10*
*Trace the symbol of the ceiba tree toward the truth of the
   curse*

Dak threw his hands in the air. "Impossible!" He didn't
have the first idea how to approach it. And usually he
was pretty good at working through the cryptic clues the
Hystorians had left so they'd know which Break to fix.

"We have to make a decision," Riq said, looking up
at Dak and Sera. "We either search for a better place to
wait out this rain, or we ignore it and concentrate on
solving the riddle."

"It's not even a question," Sera said. "We have to figure
out where we should be and what we should be doing."

"You think you can do it in these conditions?" Riq
asked.

"I know I can. We've cracked number ciphers before."

"Then let's get to work."

"Uh, guys?" Dak said. "Excuse me?" When they'd
both turned to face him, he said, "Don't you think I
should maybe have some say in this, too?"

"What is it, Dak?" Sera asked.

"Well, it's been awhile since we've eaten, right? I
mean, technically it's been several hundred years."

Sera rolled her eyes. "And your point is?"

Dak motioned to Riq. "What do you say we send
this guy off to find us a nice cheese plate? I'm thinking

Gruyère and cheddar. Maybe a few figs and grapes on the side. Oh, and saltines."

Sera's mouth fell open. "Are you kidding me right now, Dak?"

"Fine, nix the saltines," Dak said. "I get it: You're in the mood for something a bit classier. Let's go ahead and spring for TriSQuits, then."

"An absolute child," Riq said, shaking his head.

Sera and Riq both turned away from Dak and began tinkering with the SQuare. "Seriously, though," Dak called to them, "aren't you guys hungry?"

They ignored him.

Dak watched them work for a few minutes. Sera obviously knew what she was doing. She was a genius when it came to science, so working with numbers came somewhat naturally to her. And as a language whiz, Riq had an advantage over Dak whenever their clues involved codes or ciphers. Knowing that didn't make it any easier to be benched, though.

"Whatever," Dak muttered under his breath.

He wandered a few yards down the stone wall and sat against it, watching the rain and thinking about the riddle. A snake charmer. A clown. A treasure that never was. The truth of the curse. None of it rang any bells.

Being left alone like this reminded Dak of what got them into this history-saving situation in the first place. Just a few days ago — Wait, how was he supposed to measure days while traveling through time? He couldn't exactly consult a modern calendar. And the Mayan version wouldn't do him any good.

However long ago it was, the last time they were back home, in the present, he'd mistakenly let Sera into his parents' lab, where she had become obsessed with the Infinity Ring, ignoring him for hours and hours and hours — just like she was ignoring him now. Dak shook his head, thinking about that fateful day. If he'd never shown her what his parents were working on, Sera never would've figured out the missing piece of the puzzle. And if she hadn't figured out the missing piece of the puzzle, they never would've taken that stupid test run back to the Revolutionary War, and his parents wouldn't be lost somewhere in time right now.

Dak watched several more Mayas race down the white street, carrying their children in their arms. It was a strange sight considering the rain was hardly more than a lazy drizzle, though the wind was definitely picking up now.

Dak leaned his head back against the wall, fingering the iron key he had tucked into the side of his leggings. His parents had given it to him in the year 911, somehow knowing that he would need it to escape the SQ in 1850. It boggled his mind.

Dak squeezed his eyes shut, tightened his grip on the key, and imagined their faces. He understood that what he, Sera, and Riq were doing was monumentally important. They were literally trying to save the world.

And he loved warping back to different parts of history, seeing famous events unfold right before his eyes. But lately, in secret, Dak wondered if he wouldn't ditch all the heroics in exchange for having his mom and dad back in his life — even for a day.

These thoughts made Dak feel guilty, so he got up and hustled back over to Sera and Riq, saying, "Never fear, my fellow time-traveling comrades, I've come to save the day. Please, how might my talents best be utilized?"

They didn't even acknowledge his existence.

"Guys?"

Nothing.

Dak shrugged. If they didn't need him, he didn't need them either.

He turned to go and explore the wet Mayan village on his own. If he was lucky, he'd find some vital clue to the riddle . . . which he wouldn't share with anyone.

Dak found himself crossing back over the white road, toward a large domed building a little ways off. It looked like an observatory. He cupped a hand against his forehead to keep the rain out of his eyes. It was so hot and humid he was almost thankful to be wearing a breechcloth. It was actually keeping him fairly cool and allowed for occasional drafts that proved tremendously refreshing. What if he started rocking one of these bad boys in the present? Would it catch on? He pictured all his bros in fifth grade wearing them, too. Sitting around the caf, talking. Lining up for assemblies. Eventually they'd run a nice profile piece on him in the school paper next to the caption *Dak Smyth, more than your ordinary history genius.*

Then he remembered one very important fact:

He didn't really have any bros.

Unless he counted Sera—which he decided he did.

Dak tried all the doors of the observatory, but they were locked. He was surprised by the size of the building. According to his research on Mesoamerican civilizations, the Maya were curious about astrology. And art. And music. But they didn't have the technology for anything overly refined—for instance, they probably weren't spreading their cheese onto TriSQuits.

Thunder crashed so loud overhead, Dak flinched. The rain started falling harder, too, and at an odd angle.

Dak knew he should hurry back to the others, get out of the brewing storm, but just then he spotted a narrow opening in the observatory wall, like a small glassless window. He moved toward it and peered inside, the rain raking down his back. It was dark inside, except for a few candles that burned near the far wall of the large room. Next to this wall, which had a large painting of a tree, were three older men kneeling on the floor, writing on a massive sheet of a paper-like material. The thing was longer than they were tall.

Then, on the floor beside them, Dak spotted something else. A colorful mask. The kind a clown might wear. Dak immediately thought of the riddle. Maybe there was some kind of connection. And then Dak considered something else. Something potentially incredible. What if these men were working on the Great Mayan Codex? He knew there were probably many codices, a type of book, produced during this era. But his heart sped up anyway. Because everything around him made him think he was in the seventh century. And that meant it was possible that he was witnessing the composition of one of the most revered texts in all of history.

Dak pounded on the wall, so excited he was having trouble breathing. As soon as the men looked up, though, he thought better of it and ducked out of sight. Because if the authors of the Great Mayan Codex had prophesized that the SQ would one day come along and save all mankind, it was possible that the authors themselves were SQ. Or even a group of Time Wardens, whom the SQ had positioned throughout history to protect their agenda from meddling time travelers . . . like Dak.

He crouched there for several long minutes, trying to think.

Rain pummeled his entire body, puddling around his knees and elbows.

He finally pushed away from the observatory and sprinted back across the road. He had to go tell Riq and Sera about the clown mask. And the codex. Even if they didn't deserve to know.

When Dak finally rounded the stone wall and spotted his friends, he stopped in his tracks. *"No,"* he said under his breath.

Riq and Sera were surrounded by three thuggish-looking Mayas, one of whom was holding the Infinity Ring in his grimy hands.

Storm Relief

THE RAIN was pounding down so hard against the thin, metallic overhang, Riq was having trouble hearing the man standing directly in front of him. "I'm sorry, Itchik," he interrupted. "How far did you say your home is from here?"

As the man was answering, Riq caught a small blur racing toward them out of the corner of his eye. He turned to get a better look, and mumbled under his breath, "Dak?"

"Nobody messes with my friends!" Dak shouted just before launching himself at the man holding the Infinity Ring. They both fell to the ground, and the Ring went flying through the air. Riq instinctively dove out into the rain to try to catch it, but the Ring landed just beyond his reach with a thud.

"The Ring!" Sera screamed.

Riq quickly scooped it up and looked it over. It was slightly dented on one side and muddy. The screen was blank. He watched Sera position herself between Dak and the man he'd just attacked. "What in the name of mincemeat do you think you're doing?" she asked.

"Protecting you guys," Dak said.

"*Protecting* us? From what?"

"These Mayan Time Wardens!" Dak pointed at the three men.

Sera slapped a hand against her forehead.

Riq ducked back under the overhang, dripping wet. "They came out here to help us, not hurt us!" he shouted at Dak over the storm. "Itchik here was just offering to lead us to shelter."

"And how do you know it's not a trap?" Dak shouted back.

Itchik turned to Riq with a look of confusion. "What does the small boy mean 'a trap'?"

Riq sighed. "Honestly, it's best if you just ignore the small boy," he said.

Violent thunder echoed through the entire village.

"The storm!" one of the other Mayan men shouted over the increasing winds. "It is nearing the village! We must go inside immediately!"

"Please," Itchik said. "Come with us."

Riq handed the Ring back to Sera, who looked it over. "Well, let's hope it still works," she said, slipping it back into her satchel.

Riq and Sera were both staring at Dak.

"What?" he said.

The noise of the storm made it impossible to communicate.

Everyone kept quiet as the Mayas led Riq, Sera, and Dak through the bustling village. Many people seemed to be headed in the opposite direction, which worried Riq. Maybe they were following the wrong men. But when they stopped in front of an especially large stone hut, he saw other groups of Mayan families hunkering down in neighboring huts, too.

Itchik and his men quickly unlatched the front door and stepped inside, motioning for Riq and the others to enter.

"But we're sopping wet," Riq said, indicating his dripping, muddy clothes and the puddles forming around his feet.

"This does not matter," Itchik said. "Please, you must join us inside."

As they wrung out their clothes by the door, Riq peered around the inside of the hut. He trusted Itchik and his friends, but he also couldn't shake the memory of what had happened in 1850, when SQ slave traders had masqueraded as Hystorian allies. His eyes went immediately to a cluster of Mayas huddled together in the middle of the room, singing. Based on the lyrics, Riq gathered that their song was directed at some type of rain god. He studied their faces, which showed both fear and awe for the storm.

A girl around his age suddenly turned and met his eyes. She was still singing with everyone else, but he noticed a slight raise at the corners of her mouth. This subtle smile made him feel that he was safe inside the hut. But it also made him feel something else. Something he couldn't quite put his finger on.

The girl turned back to the group just as Dak whispered, "Guys, listen to me. I don't think they're Time Wardens."

Sera patted him on the back. "Whatever gives you that idea, Dak? Is it because that's what we just told you outside? Or is it the fact that they basically rescued us from a tropical storm?"

"And brought us into their home," Riq added.

Dak frowned at Riq and turned back to Sera. "Look, I'm sorry I damaged the Ring, okay? But I saw these guys huddled around you, and one of them was holding the Ring, and I just sort of freaked."

Sera sighed. "Don't worry, we'll fix it," she said. "I'll fix it."

"At least I figured out what time we're in," Dak said. "Approximately. We're definitely in the seventh century, not 1562. We were off by less than a millennium."

"That part is my fault," Sera whispered. "Although I'm not sure what I did wrong."

"I'm still not convinced landing here was a mistake," Riq replied. "Maybe there's something important happening here, too. Like, what if this storm is somehow connected to the riddle?"

"Oh, oh, oh." Dak was suddenly so excited he was jumping up and down. "I meant to tell you guys. I saw something important inside the observatory. You won't believe this. Seriously."

"Go on," Sera said. "Spit it out."

But before Dak could say another word, Itchik clapped his hands together and called to them. "Friends, please join us in our small ceremony. We are asking the gods not to wash away our crops. And for a safe passage here for our neighbors from Calakmul, who are to come and study our discoveries."

Riq motioned for Sera and Dak to follow him toward the middle of the room. As they walked, Dak said softly, "I'll tell you guys about the observatory later. It could be part of the riddle, though. Also, I have a new theory about these people. I think they might be Hystorians."

"They're not Hystorians," Riq said, turning around.

"How do you know?"

"We sort of asked them already," Sera said. "Indirectly, of course."

Dak shook his head. "No, I definitely think they're Hystorians. Why else would they be so much nicer than the history books portray them?"

Riq tuned out of the rest of Dak and Sera's whispered conversation. He was too busy testing a theory of his own. He stared at the Mayan girl who had smiled at him, willing her to turn and look at him one more time. He needed to see how he reacted.

It took a few seconds, but she finally did turn to him, still singing, and looked directly into his eyes. And she gave him another smile, too—a real one this time.

Riq's suspicions were confirmed.

The second their eyes locked, that strange feeling returned to his stomach. It was almost like a Remnant, but better, somehow. A good kind of queasiness. What did it mean? Whatever the answer, it was unlike anything Riq had ever felt before.

4

The Wrath of Chaac

WHILE EVERYONE else was chanting to the Mayan rain deity, Chaac, Sera was quietly experiencing the most profound Remnant of her entire life. Her stomach was twisted in knots. She clenched her teeth and cringed at the familiar iron taste flooding her mouth. She felt so dizzy she had to plant both hands firmly on the dirt floor next to where she sat.

Dak and Riq were totally unaware. They'd just been taught the simple refrain and had joined the Mayas in their chanting. The man who called himself Itchik was the only one who seemed to notice Sera's distress. Thankfully, he wasn't calling attention to it.

Sera was all too familiar with Remnants—the feeling that something was missing, that if history had unfolded in a slightly different way she'd be living her real life instead of this shadow version. Back home, she'd often walk past her barn and suddenly be overwhelmed by the sense that her parents, who she'd never known, were inside, tending to a trio of beautiful Thoroughbreds. But when she pulled open the door, she'd find the barn completely empty.

Her Remnants had grown stronger since they started traveling through time, but this was by far the most powerful one she had experienced. She took deep, even breaths, wondering why now. During a storm. Surrounded by Mayas.

When the Remnant finally passed, Sera let out a relieved sigh and resumed halfheartedly mouthing the chant with everyone else. She noted how intensely the storm was hammering down on the roof above them, the sound echoing throughout the cavernous hut. She studied the worried look on all the faces around her. The storm was much more severe than she had thought it would be—though it was nothing compared to what she remembered of the Cataclysm.

After a few more minutes, Itchik raised a hand and the chanting ceased.

"Young visitors from a faraway place," he said, "I would like to welcome you to our village and introduce you to my people." He proceeded to rattle off several Mayan names that Sera knew she'd never remember—especially on the heels of such a powerful Remnant. There were three separate Mayan families, each with several children. There were a few stooped elders, too. The only name that stuck in Sera's head was "Kisa," the girl who was a few years older than Sera and very pretty.

Itchik turned to his people and said, "And this is Riq,

Sera, and . . . I'm sorry, I don't believe I ever learned the name of the smaller boy."

"I'm not that small!" Dak fired back.

"It's a pleasure meeting everyone," Riq blurted out.

Sera leaned over to Dak and whispered, "Try to keep in mind that if it wasn't for them, we'd be out there getting pummeled by this storm."

Dak turned to Itchik. "The name's Dak Smyth, sir dude."

"Very good," Itchik said. "My family and I would like to welcome all of you to our home."

"Welcome," everyone else said together.

One of the women unpacked a small stack of asymmetrical tortilla-looking things and passed them out to everyone. Sera didn't realize how hungry she was until she started eating the corn-based bread.

Minutes later, there was a loud crashing sound on the roof, and everyone looked up. "What was that?" the girl named Kisa said.

"The storm still grows," one of the elders explained. "Trees are now blowing over."

Two small girls began to cry quietly and ducked under the arms of their mother.

"Don't be scared," the elder said. "Chaac is looking over us."

Itchik turned to Sera, Dak, and Riq and said, "From where have you traveled, friends? You certainly don't look like our neighbors to the north or south." He paused for a second and pointed at Sera. "With the exception of the girl."

"I'm definitely not your neighbor," she snapped.

Riq shot her a look.

Sera shrugged. Even Riq would have to admit that associating her with the Maya didn't make sense. And back in second grade, during a lesson on lost civilizations, stupid Sylvia Walker had drawn a stick figure of a girl sitting on top of a Mayan temple next to the caption *Sera's great great-great-grandmother.* The kids all laughed and asked if her mom packed a thermos full of goat blood in her lunch.

There was a reason Sera was so sensitive

"Where are we from?" Dak echoed. He had a big grin on his face, which told Sera she should be extremely worried. "That's an interesting question, Itchy."

"Itchik," Riq corrected.

Dak winked at Sera and Riq and turned back to the Mayan man.

"We come from a place far, far away. . . . I believe you know what I'm saying."

"The remote highlands?" Itchik asked.

"Dak," Sera said, shooting him a dirty look. "We've already discussed this—"

"Let me put it another way," Dak said, ignoring her. "You know your fancy calendar?"

"Ah, one of the great achievements of our ancestors," Itchik said.

"Yeah, well, we've just about made it to the end of that bad boy."

Sera looked to Riq, who let his head fall into his hands.

Itchik was staring at Dak, a confused look on his face.

"Where do we come from?" Dak said. "Let's just say it's a place where people consider *these* things a little outdated." He pointed down at his breechcloth.

"Seriously, Dak," Sera tried again. "Drop it. Please." Dak couldn't seem to get it through his thick head that not everyone they met was going to be a Hystorian or Time Warden.

Dak only grinned at Sera and turned back to Itchik. "I'm talking about the future, Itchy. Where people drive cars and fly planes and eat tortillas that are actually symmetrical. Filled with grated cheese. I'm talking about quesadillas, my friend."

Sera rolled her eyes. She glanced at Riq, who threw his hands in the air.

"I don't understand what your friend is saying," Itchik said, turning to them.

"Neither does he," Sera answered. "Please, just ignore—"

"Do I really have to spell this thing out for everybody?" Dak interrupted. "You guys are *Hy-stor-i-ans*. And we've traveled here from the *fu-ture*. Go on, Sera. Show him the Infinity Ring again and explain how it works. Riq, pull the riddle up on the SQuare. I can't believe I have to broker this whole thing myself."

"What's a Hystorian?" Kisa asked.

Everyone was staring at Dak, completely baffled, including Sera and Riq.

Even the smallest Mayan baby was staring at him.

The grin on Dak's face slowly fell away and he turned to Sera. "Wait, is it possible that they're not actually Hystorians?"

Before Sera could answer there was a second tremendous crashing sound from up above. Sera looked up and saw that the wooden slats were actually being pulled from the roof and carried away in the powerful winds. Rain started streaming down into the hut, scattering everyone. The children screamed, and their parents covered their small heads and hurried them to the far wall, away from the widening hole.

Sera, Dak, and Riq ran to the opposite corner.

"The storm is too vicious!" Riq shouted. "The entire roof will come down!"

Sera looked up. She saw more wood being torn away. Uneven chunks of rock came crashing down into the hut. "We can't stay here!" she shouted. But when she tried to get up, Riq held her by the wrist.

"We need to stick together!" he shouted.

There was so much commotion inside the disintegrating hut, Sera couldn't think. Rain poured down all around them. The wind howled. Children wailed. A thick tree branch fell from above, slamming into the earth only inches in front of Sera's face.

"Watch out!" Dak suddenly shouted.

Sera thought he was shouting at her, but when she looked up she saw a little Mayan girl standing alone near the front door of the hut, crying, as that part of the wall started caving in. Before Sera could even think to move, Dak sprang to his feet and raced toward the girl. He shoved her out of harm's way, toward her mom, just as the wall collapsed, cracking him in the back of the head and driving him into the ground.

"Dak!" Sera screamed.

She sprinted over to him, slid down to her knees, and lifted his face. He was trapped under the rubble of the stone wall, and his eyes were huge with fear. There was already blood caked in his hair, running in slick lines down his neck and shoulders.

"Dak!" she shouted again. "Dak, please! Can you hear me?"

"The observatory," he mumbled.

"What?"

"The people writing inside," he said, blinking his eyes and swallowing. "See them. It could be part of the riddle."

"I don't understand what you're saying," Sera pleaded.

Riq was beside them now, too.

"Stay with me, Dak!" Sera shouted. "Just stay with me!"

But Dak's eyes slowly rolled into the back of his head. He lost consciousness.

A Sleepless Night

RIQ STRAINED to keep a tight grip under both of Dak's arms as he helped carry him through the surging storm. Itchik and another man had his feet. He watched Sera hurrying alongside them, holding a blanket over Dak's face so he wouldn't drown in the falling rain. "Dak!" she kept shouting. "Can you hear me, Dak? It's Sera! Please look at me, Dak!"

But Dak wasn't looking at anyone.

He was out cold.

Riq had never seen anyone take such a nasty blow in his life.

As they moved past the temple, a sudden gust of wind knocked them all over into the mud. Riq and the two Mayan men scrambled to their feet, quickly lifting Dak back up and continuing away from the village, toward the hills on the outskirts of town. The women, children, and elders from the hut were several paces ahead already, holding on to one another, leaning into the teeth of the storm.

Riq winced as he slowly moved through the mud with Dak. His leg was killing him. He'd been struck in the knee by a falling board when the roof of the hut had collapsed. He wasn't sure how much longer he could go on. But every time he thought of asking for a rest, he would picture Dak pushing that little girl out of the way, taking the brunt of the wall's impact on his own head and back.

He'd saved her life.

Remembering this fact always gave Riq the shot of adrenaline he needed to fight through the pain and fatigue.

They carried Dak uphill over fallen trees, through knee-high puddles of rain, and across long stretches of quicksand-like mud. Eventually they approached the mouth of a large cave, where several Mayan warriors were perched on large boulders watching the storm.

Itchik shouted at the men, "Get Jasaw immediately! We must help this boy!"

Two of the warriors darted inside the cave. The rest leaped down from the boulders, into the rain, and helped carry Dak's limp body up to the cave's broad opening.

Riq was relieved of his grip on Dak once they got inside. He watched Itchik and the others carry Dak across the dimly lit cave, Sera trailing closely behind. It took Riq's eyes a few seconds to adjust to the dull candlelight, but once he could see, he was taken aback.

Several hundred Mayas were spread out on blankets across the uneven floor of the cave. Some were sleeping. Others were sitting together in small groups, chanting. A few turned to look him over.

A man wearing a headdress pointed the men carrying Dak toward a large hanging blanket, set up like a screen for privacy. Riq knew this must be the man Itchik had referred to as Jasaw, and he hurried to catch up. When he ducked behind the blanket, he saw the men lowering Dak onto a cot. There were other patients on cots nearby. Riq was relieved they'd made it out of the storm, to a place where Dak might get help, and only now did he reach down to massage his aching knee. When he brought his fingers back up to his face, he saw blood. The board had cut him.

Riq moved toward Dak's cot, nodding to the men who had helped carry Dak as they left.

"Who are you anyway?" Sera was asking the man looking over Dak's wounds.

"I am Jasaw," he said without looking up. "The *ahmen*, medicine man, of our village. Your friend is very hurt."

"And how do *you* know how hurt he is?" Sera said. "It's not like you're a real doctor."

"What is 'doctor'?" Jasaw said, looking up at her.

Riq placed his hand on Sera's arm to try to calm her down. "How bad are his injuries?" he asked Jasaw.

The man turned his focus back to Dak and shook his

head. He ran his hands lightly over Dak's face and neck, and then left them hovering over his eyes, as if he was trying to read something through his palms. Then he leaned an ear against Dak's chest. "Something has struck your friend on the head, yes?"

Riq and Sera both nodded.

"He is breathing normally, but I fear his brain may swell, which would be very bad." Riq watched the man grind up several different kinds of herbs, stir them into a liquid that looked like wine, and drip some of the concoction onto Dak's tongue. Then he rubbed his hands together and touched Dak's head and back. "No broken bones," he said.

"How do you know?" Sera said. "You don't have an X-ray machine. You don't have anything!"

"Sera," Riq said. "He's doing the best he can."

"I have what I need," Jasaw said.

Sera turned to Riq. "We have to get him to a hospital. Now." Riq could see the fear flickering in Sera's eyes.

"But Itchik says he's the best," Riq told her.

"The best what?" Sera said. "The best mystic?"

"Healer."

"Dak needs a real doctor," Sera said. "You saw that wall fall on him."

Riq rubbed Sera's shoulder. "We can't chance warping out of here with Dak unconscious. You said it yourself: It's getting harder and harder on our bodies. We have to wait until he's stronger."

Jasaw was now pushing his hands up Dak's chest, toward his face.

"What are you doing?" Sera asked him.

"Ridding the body of evil spirits," Jasaw said without looking up.

Sera shot Riq a desperate look. "I'm staying right here," she said. "All night. I'm making sure he takes care of Dak."

Jasaw burned a plant-based incense over Dak's body. The smell was strong. Riq knew Sera didn't believe in anything spiritual like this. She believed in hard science. But this was Dak's only hope.

He pictured what happened again. Dak rushing into the middle of the hut, pushing the girl to safety, the wall coming down on the back of his head. Riq leaned in close to Dak's ear and said in a quiet voice that even Sera wouldn't be able to hear, "You saved that girl's life, Dak. You know that? You're a hero."

He kept waiting for Dak to open his eyes and say something sarcastic.

But he never did.

He just lay there, completely still, as Jasaw rubbed dark ash onto his forehead.

Riq tried sleeping on the blanket Itchik set out for him, but he was unable to shut off his mind. He kept picturing the stone wall coming down on

Dak and the cryptic riddle they'd pulled up on the SQuare. He also thought about his time on the run in 1850. He'd been able to keep a young boy, James, out of the hands of slave traders. Why was he so helpless now?

Eventually, he gave up on sleep. He walked quietly over to the cave opening and sat on a boulder to watch the powerful storm. The rain still poured down on the beautiful green Mayan landscape. The wind still whipped through the trees. But the thunder and lightning seemed more distant now, which told Riq the worst of it had passed.

Riq had always been intrigued by natural disasters. In an odd way, sometimes he even found himself rooting for storms and earthquakes and tornados. It's not that he wanted to see anyone get hurt, and he knew the increased frequency of these disasters was a direct result of the SQ creating Breaks in history — the Breaks he, Dak, and Sera were busy trying to correct. But he always thought that maybe the right disaster would come along and hit the SQ where it hurt, compromising their political power. Maybe it would be like hitting the RESET button on the world.

But there was a non-SQ-related reason he was so fascinated by disasters, too. A reason nobody who knew him would ever suspect. Secretly, Riq sometimes wanted to hit the RESET button on his own life.

For as long as he could remember, he'd worked tirelessly to be the best at everything he did. School, soccer, language acquisition, The Art of Memory . . . At first it was fun, and the praise he received made him feel special. But somewhere along the line, things shifted. The fun faded. The pressure to stay on top started weighing down on his shoulders. He put in all those extra hours not because he was enjoying himself, but because he was afraid to fail. Lately, he had been having an awful recurring nightmare where Brint and Mari followed him around, shaking their heads in disappointment. His classmates spoke in hushed voices about him getting only an A minus.

Riq was watching the pouring rain, dreaming about living a normal life where he'd sleep in on weekends and hang out at the mall, when he heard footsteps creeping up behind him.

He spun around quickly, instinctively popping to his feet. It was Kisa.

"Hey," she said, grinning at his military move.

"Hey," Riq said back, slowly unclenching his fists.

"I can't sleep either." She was holding a small wooden box in her right hand. "I keep thinking about what happened to your friend. I'm really sorry."

Riq nodded.

"Jasaw is a gifted healer, though. He'll make sure your friend has the best care."

"Thanks," Riq said. He searched his mind for something else to say. But he didn't have any experience talking to girls like Kisa so he sort of just stood there awkwardly, looking at her.

"What about you?" she said. "How's your knee?"

He furrowed his brow, confused. "How'd you know I hurt my knee?"

She switched the wooden box from her right hand to her left. "I saw you limping while you were carrying your friend. And then in the cave you were rubbing it. You should really tell Jasaw what happened."

"I'll be okay," Riq said. "It's just a cut." He looked at her for a few long seconds trying to think of something else to say, something that would keep her out here with him, but his mind felt sluggish and his stomach had that weird feeling again.

"Mind if I sit out here for a bit?" she asked.

"Yes," he said, a little too excitedly. "I mean, no, I don't mind—yes, you can sit." He felt heat rising into his cheeks and the tips of his ears.

Kisa sat on the boulder next to his and set down her wooden box.

"What's in there?" Riq asked.

"Jewelry," she said. "I figured if I was going to have a sleepless night, I might as well get some work done."

Riq watched her remove a small block of wood and a knife and start whittling.

"My mother says it's a man's job to make artistic things," she said. "But I know my jewelry's as good as any man's, if not better." She looked up at Riq. "I hate that there are things girls aren't supposed to be good at. Who says?"

Kisa pulled a metal piece out of her box and held it up for Riq to see.

He took the bracelet and turned it over in his hands. "Wow," he said. It was shaped like a thin, coiled snake. Each scale was meticulously crafted, as were the eyes and tongue. It was as well constructed as any piece of jewelry he'd seen in the modern world. "I'm impressed," he told her, handing back the snake.

Kisa smiled and put it away. "Can I ask you something, Riq? I've been wondering about it all night."

"Of course," he said.

"What's a Hystorian?"

He studied her dark brown eyes. During training back home, his supervisors drilled into him the importance of guarding Hystorian intel. Even the daily cafeteria menu was password protected. But Riq was weary from all the time travel. And the storm. And what had happened to Dak. He needed to talk to someone.

So he did.

He told Kisa about the SQ and Aristotle's theory about the Great Breaks. He explained how the world was thrown off balance every time history had been altered by the SQ, causing strange occurrences all over, far worse than this storm. He told her Hystorians were people stationed throughout time, trained to look out for the time travelers Aristotle predicted would one day show up from the future to try to fix history and save the world.

When he finished, Kisa looked at him for a long time before saying, "So you three really are from the future? Like your friend said?"

Riq knew he'd said too much already. He expected this to make him feel tremendously guilty, but it didn't. For whatever reason, he trusted Kisa.

"It's okay," she said. "You don't have to answer that." She went back to whittling away at her piece of wood.

Riq could now see what she was carving. A snake rising up out of a basket. "Can I ask you a question now, Kisa?"

She nodded.

"Did you live in the hut that was destroyed?"

"No," she said. "But I spent a lot of time there. My uncle Itchik lived there with his family."

"How will he fix it? And where will everyone live in the meantime?"

"Someone will take them in," she said. "We all look out for one another in my village."

They talked for a while longer, mostly about Kisa's family and her village. Riq was moved by how much they cared for one another. And how much they respected the land. They seemed far different from the way they were presented in history classes. And he was surprised to find out that Itchik was no ordinary man. He was the king of Izamal. Had been for years.

Then they sat together in silence, Kisa whittling and Riq watching the rain soften and the dark slowly lose its grip on the sky. It felt nice sitting beside her without talking. He didn't feel awkward anymore.

Eventually, Kisa packed up her things and stood and wished Riq a good night. But she didn't leave right away. She just stood there, watching the quiet rainfall for a few moments. "One day," she finally said, turning to Riq, "I want to do something special, too."

"I bet you will," he said.

She smiled, then turned and walked back into the cave.

It wasn't until Kisa was long gone that Riq noticed she'd left the snake bracelet on the boulder where she'd been sitting. He was about to scoop it up and hurry after her, but then he saw the message she'd carved into the rock. He stared at the glyphs for several seconds. He was one of the few Hystorians who could decipher Mayan writing, but it wasn't easy. Eventually, he was able to read: *For my new friend, Riq.*

He slipped the bracelet onto his wrist, feeling a wave of excitement pass through his body. He lifted the piece of jewelry up to his eyes to study the details of the metallic snake — and then a thought suddenly occurred to him.

What if Kisa was the snake charmer from the riddle?

6

The Symbol of the Ceiba Tree

SERA CONTINUED down the hill beside Riq, overcome with guilt about leaving Dak's side. Her best friend still hadn't regained consciousness, and she wanted to be the first thing he saw when he opened his eyes. And who knew what crazy potion that mystic might try without her supervision? But when Riq had stirred her from a restless sleep, he reminded her of Dak's last words about the people inside the observatory. The least they could do, he reasoned, was honor their friend's wishes by checking it out.

So here Sera was.

Trekking down to the observatory.

The guilt tightening like a noose around her neck with each step she took away from the cave.

"I mean, just look at it," Riq continued. "It's incredible what Kisa was able to do without the help of modern tools."

"Wow, it really is," Sera said, rolling her eyes. Riq hadn't stopped talking about Kisa and his new bracelet since they started their walk. He'd already explained his theory about her being the snake charmer from the riddle. He believed she might hold the key to discovering the Break they needed to fix. He described for Sera the deep conversation he'd had with Kisa, which had lasted into the morning. Now he was obsessing over the artistic merits of the bracelet she'd given him. Riq was so caught up in Kisa talk, he didn't even seem to notice all the storm damage they were passing. The thick tree branches strewn all over the dirt path. The massive reddish brown puddles and blown-off roofs. The smaller huts on the outskirts of the village that had been completely flattened.

"And it's surprisingly comfortable," Riq said, spinning the bracelet around his wrist for Sera to see. "I never thought of myself as a bracelet-wearing kind of guy, but this thing's a different deal. I really dig it."

"I'm sure you do." Sera hadn't known Riq long, but she was willing to go out on a limb and say he was acting out of character. Not that she had time to worry about Riq's character at the moment. Her focus was on getting to the observatory, finding out whatever it was they were supposed to find out, then getting back up to the cave to check on Dak.

When Sera looked up a few minutes later, her eyes

grew big and she stopped in her tracks. The observatory.

Riq turned around. "I bet Kisa would make you some-thing, too, if—"

"Look!" Sera interrupted, pointing ahead of them. Yesterday the observatory had been nearly as tall as the temple. Now Sera was staring at a heap of rubble.

"The storm," Riq said under his breath.

Sera's body went cold. Most of the roof had been stripped away. The walls were folded in on one another and crumbling near the base. A dozen men, including Itchik, were standing on top of the wreckage, calling out names and carrying debris away, stone by stone.

Sera and Riq took off running down the hill.

Sera quickly learned that there were three elders trapped inside: Cocom, Kan Boar, and Pacal. They were the reason everyone was working at such a fran-tic pace. Itchik kept calling out their names and digging through the rubble, trying to determine the location of the voices that occasionally echoed back. Sera and Riq worked right alongside the Mayas.

Initially, there were a dozen Mayan men helping out. Then two dozen. Then three. All of them hoisted boulders nearly as big as their own bodies. Women started pitching in. Older children. By late afternoon there were over two hundred people milling around the observatory wreckage, carrying away rocks. Those too young or old to lift debris ladled fresh water from buckets into cups and passed out fruit to those who'd been working since morning and refused to take a break. Nearly every face Sera had seen in the cave the night before was out here now, helping to dig the elders out from under the debris.

Soon the sun started to set, but that didn't slow the Mayas. So it didn't slow Sera either. She lifted as many smaller stones as she could manage, carrying them to one of several piles of rubble near the temple. Riq did the same, Kisa now working at his side. Sera occasionally scanned the crowd for Dak, hoping he'd woken up and demanded to join the rescue efforts. She knew that's exactly what he'd do.

But there was no sign of him.

"Cocom!" Itchik continued to roar. "Kan Boar! Pacal!"

"Who are these people anyway?" Sera asked Riq and Kisa as she tossed two grapefruit-size rocks onto the pile of rubble.

"Wise men, right?" Riq said, turning to Kisa.

Kisa wiped sweat from her brow and nodded. "They are the scribes of our village."

"Why were they in the observatory during the storm?" Sera asked as the three of them started back toward the wreckage site.

"Only Itchik knows for sure," Kisa said. "Though many believe they were working on a secret project to be studied by the men of Yuknoom the Great, king of

Calakmul. His men will be visiting our village in a few days' time."

"I still can't believe Itchik is a king," Sera said, recalling what Riq had told her on the way down the hill. "He never even let on last night."

"He is our king," Kisa said, "but more important, according to Itchik himself, he is a father and husband and uncle."

Sera nodded, but she was having trouble wrapping her head around these Mayas compared to the Maya she'd read about. Itchik didn't set himself apart from everyone. She thought that's what all kings did. And it moved her to see everyone pitching in to help rescue the trapped elders.

When Kisa broke off to get a cup of water, Sera took Riq by the arm. "Did you ask her about the riddle?"

He nodded. "In a roundabout way. Apparently, when she was little she survived a bite from the dead-liest snake in the lowlands. Her uncle said she needed to honor the snake for not taking her life. That's the reason she works snakes into her jewelry. Seems weird for it to just be a coincidence. I'll keep working on it."

Sera let out a defeated sigh. "What are we doing here, Riq? Dak's hurt, and the Ring is malfunctioning, and we aren't getting any closer to understanding the riddle. I'm so confused."

"I am, too, Sera. We just have to keep searching."

Sera saw Kisa approaching with two cups of water. At least Riq had made a friend, she thought. Which made her think of poor Dak, laid up in a dingy cave, alone.

Kisa handed a cup to both Riq and Sera, and they thanked her.

As Sera finished her water, she heard a small commotion building on the other side of the rubble. She set down her cup next to Riq's and Kisa's, and the three of them hurried around the wreckage, toward a gathering crowd.

"What's happening?" Kisa asked a stocky Mayan woman.

"They've spotted the scribes underneath the wreckage," the woman said excitedly. "They're alive!"

Sera pushed her way around several people to see for herself.

Itchik was right up front calling out, "Pacal, remain calm! We will get you out of there!" He turned to the group of men next to him and said, "It's a miracle they're not harmed. Now let's hurry."

It took another hour to clear a wide enough tunnel for the scribes to climb out of. Sera watched them emerge, one by one, dirty but otherwise unscathed. The last man who came out was carrying a large tablet of bark-colored paper, which was filled with strange-looking glyphs and paintings. He handed the tablet to Itchik, who looked it over, saying, "How did you survive, Pacal?"

Pacal pointed back at the tunnel. "We huddled next

to the wall with the ceiba tree. It saved our lives."

Itchik smiled and nodded, looking back and forth between the three filthy men and the tablet. "It is our good luck charm as always," he said.

"While we were trapped, I decided I will paint the tree onto the first and last pages of the codex," Pacal said. "I believe it will be a worthy addition."

"Yes, absolutely."

Sera couldn't believe what she was seeing. An actual Mayan codex. She ducked down so she could peer into the narrow hole. It was dark inside, but once her eyes adjusted she was able to make out the large tree painted on the wall. She got goose bumps and quickly turned to Riq. "The riddle!"

"I was thinking the same thing," he said.

It was late by the time Sera made it back to the cave and Dak's bedside. He was still unresponsive, though Jasaw seemed to think his condition had improved. Sera wasn't so sure. If anything, Dak's injuries looked worse. There was a lump the size of a softball on the back of his head. The backs of his arms and shoulders were entirely black and blue.

"He looks awful," Sera said.

"It is not important how he appears on the outside," Jasaw said, waving more incense over Dak's bare chest. "It is his insides that matter. And there is no longer a danger of his brain swelling."

Sera stared at Dak. She was beginning to trust Jasaw a little more, though she still wished he could back up his claims with an MRI.

Once Jasaw left, Sera pulled out the SQuare and powered it on. She and Riq had ducked behind a huge tree outside the village to study the riddle before trekking back to the cave. But even knowing that the symbol of the ceiba tree was part of this local codex, they were just as lost.

The riddle came up, and she read it aloud to Dak, over and over, hoping something would jump out at her:

A snake charmer and a clown
A treasure that never was
A gift from the deity Itzamna: from 9.10.5.10.7 to
    11.17.2.13.10
Trace the symbol of the ceiba tree toward the truth of the
    curse

Sera read each phrase a dozen times, but they still didn't add up to anything. And Dak just lay there, unmoving.

Next, she booted up the Ring. She had been able to get the display working again, but something was still wrong. The Ring wouldn't accept any new data. Every time she input new coordinates, she got an error message. It was deeply troubling.

Eventually, she shut off both machines, curled up on the ground next to Dak's cot, and closed her eyes. She pushed Dak and the riddle out of her mind, and instead focused on her trip to the Cataclysm. She remembered the flooding streets. The bloodred sun. But as soon as she saw herself reaching for the doorknob of her house, things went blank.

Again.

What had she seen that was so awful her mind wouldn't let her remember?

A New Purpose

RIQ STOPPED pacing and looked over Sera's shoulder as she continued tinkering with the Infinity Ring. He sensed her frustration, and he wished there was more he could do to help. But she was operating on a level of physics that was simply beyond him. They'd been huddled behind the cave like this for several hours already, and it didn't seem like they were any closer to a solution. She'd gotten the screen to come back on, but all it did was flash a series of error messages.

Riq resumed his nervous pacing. He needed to get down to the village and find Kisa. During another sleepless night he had decided to ask for her help with the riddle. It went against every Hystorian principle he'd ever been taught, but he was going to show it to her. Maybe she'd be able to decipher something that he and Sera weren't seeing.

Sera placed the Ring onto the thick grass and clenched her fists. "I've figured out what's wrong," she said. "But you're not going to like it."

"What is it?" Riq asked.

"Basically, the Ring rebooted when it hit the ground. Everything is still operational . . . except the Ring 'forgot' what the date is. It doesn't know when we are. And if it doesn't have that data, it can't warp us out of here. It doesn't know what our starting point is."

"That's not so bad," Riq said. "We just have to figure out the date?"

"Think about it," Sera said. "The Maya have a calendar system, sure. But it's different from ours. The Ring's programming is all based on a European calendar. And the Mayan people have had no contact with Europeans."

"We'll get it, Sera." Riq figured it was a good idea to put a positive spin on things. "Even if we have to cross the ocean to do it."

Sera shook her head, staring at the Ring.

After a long silence, she picked it back up and resumed her tinkering. Riq watched, knowing he couldn't tell her the other thing he'd been thinking about all night. How he wouldn't mind being stuck here for another day or two. There was something genuinely special about this place.

And while he knew their mission was crucial, Riq wasn't exactly in a hurry to return home.

He hadn't told the others yet. Maybe he never would. But their visit to 1850 had cost Riq a great deal. He had been forced to interfere with his own family tree, and that meant he was pretty sure he had no family left in the present day. It also meant he could cease to exist if he ever returned to the twenty-first century. He wasn't sure which possibility scared him more.

He was doing a good job of keeping his emotions in check, but all the uncertainty had hit him the previous afternoon, while he and Kisa were helping clear debris from the site of the observatory. Suddenly, these thoughts had hit Riq so hard he had lowered himself into the mud and covered his face with his hands.

Kisa had knelt beside him and patted him on the back and asked if he was okay. But that was it. She didn't press him for details. She understood that there were things about him she would never understand. And she accepted it. And wasn't that what true friendship was all about?

Riq realized two things in that moment:

One: Not counting his fellow time travelers, he'd never had a real friend before—other than his grandma.

And two: If Kisa was a real friend, then he should be able to trust her with the riddle.

Sera threw her hands in the air. "I have no idea what else to try, Riq. What if we're stuck here forever?"

Riq paused a few seconds, thinking about this. How would he feel if they were stuck here forever? The idea didn't bother him nearly as much as it should. "Look," he said, forcing himself to focus, "why don't we forget about the Ring for now and concentrate on the riddle? If we go down to the village, we can ask

Itchik about the ceiba tree. And I have a few questions for Kisa, too."

The worried look on Sera's face made Riq feel guilty. He'd never seen her so distraught.

"Maybe you're right," she said, slipping the Ring back into her satchel. "Let me check on Dak and then we can go."

They stumbled into Itchik as soon as they'd made it into the village. He was standing at the foot of the fallen observatory, laughing.

"Itchik?" Riq said.

Itchik turned to look at Riq and Sera, his grin falling from his face. "How is your friend? His condition is improving, I hope."

"Jasaw claims he's getting better," Sera answered. "But he's still unresponsive."

Itchik nodded. "My entire family owes him a debt of gratitude. That was my youngest daughter he pushed out of the way."

"What are you doing out here?" Riq asked. It seemed more than a little odd that a king would be laughing at his own fallen observatory. "Everything okay?"

"Oh, yes." Itchik turned back to the rubble and said, "I was just thinking about how long it took us to build. Many years. The entire village pitched in. We made many important discoveries about the world from inside these walls."

"Why were you laughing, then?" Sera said.

"My scribes were not harmed," Itchik said. "And I believe one's greatest misfortune is also his greatest opportunity. We will build a new observatory now. One that is bigger and better. One that will not fall, no matter how hard the wind blows."

Riq wished he could have this kind of attitude about life, too. But it was easier said than done. He looked all around the village, at the series of storm-damaged huts people were already attempting to rebuild, the towering temple, the muddied white road. There had to be a reason Riq, Dak, and Sera had come here. It couldn't be a random mistake. What if they'd come here specifically for Riq? So he could meet these people and see how they live and hear what they believe?

Riq looked up when he heard voices. He spotted a group of children hurrying down the path toward them.

"King Itchik!" they called in unison. "King Itchik!"

Itchik and Sera looked up, too. Riq saw that there was a smaller group trailing behind the children. Older kids. Teens like him. One of them was Kisa.

"King Itchik!"

"Yes, children, what is it?" Itchik asked.

A boy at the head of the pack spoke. "The men have arrived from the jungle!" he said, out of breath as they reached the foot of the fallen observatory. "King Yuknoom's men. From Calakmul!"

"They've come days earlier than expected," Itchik said. "Where are they now, children?"

"The north ball court," the biggest Mayan boy said.

Itchik turned to Riq and Sera. "I must go greet the great king's men," he said. "They have come to appraise our learning. You are welcome to meet them, too." He started following the children back the other way.

Riq and Sera looked at each other. "I'm going with him," Sera said. "Maybe I can find out more about the codex."

"I'll meet you there later," Riq said.

Sera nodded and hurried to catch up with the group heading toward the ball court. Riq moved toward Kisa. Before he could even open his mouth to ask to speak with her, she took his arm and told him, "Come with me."

Kisa pulled him into an empty hut that no longer had a roof. This hut was much smaller than the one Riq had visited during the great storm. "I don't trust these men," Kisa told him as soon as they were alone.

"The king's people?" Riq asked. "Why not?"

"Itchik believes they want to study our codex so they can learn from it. But he's too trusting. I believe they want to steal our work and claim it as their own. Everyone knows Pacal is the best scribe in any village."

Riq looked out the open door. Several older Mayan women were in an organized line sweeping the road.

Men were moving in and out of other huts with ancient-looking tools. "Shouldn't we warn Itchik?" he said, turning back to Kisa.

"He won't listen. All he cares about is proving our progress to others." Kisa took Riq's arm. "You need to be careful, too," she said. "And the smaller boy who was hurt. They have been known to capture people who look different. I heard they take them back to Calakmul and shove them in cages. People pay to view them."

"Trust me," Riq said, remembering his experiences in 1850, "nobody's putting me in a cage."

Kisa nodded and picked up one of the ceiling boards lying by her feet. She stared at it for a few seconds and then turned to Riq with glassy eyes. "I guess I'm just worried for the people I care about. This storm has ruined so many of our homes. And our observatory. Everyone is working hard to recover. And here come these men from the richest village in the lowlands, demanding to see the fruit of our learning. It doesn't seem right."

"I wish I could be more help," Riq said.

Kisa shook her head. "You have your own worries."

Riq focused on the ground, thinking. No matter what happened to him, he needed to make sure Dak and Sera were okay. He needed to make sure the Hystorians' mission didn't end here. He pulled the SQuare out of his satchel and looked up at Kisa.

He waited for her to ask what it was, but she just

stared at it, watching him push the power button. "I was wondering if you'd look at something for me," he said.

"Of course," she told him. "But I've never seen anything like that. I may not be any help."

He typed in the password and pulled up the riddle, then held the screen up for Kisa to see. When she gave him a blank look, he blushed. Of course she couldn't read it. It was written in English. He translated for her verbally.

"This is why you asked about snakes in my jewelry," Kisa said.

Riq nodded. "Do any of the lines make sense to you?"

"I don't know what the clown could be. Or the treasure. But I know Itzamna, of course. He is the god who gave us our calendar. And the numbers you read, those are calendar dates. One of them is today. The other is far into the future. Knowing one, it is a simple matter to deduce the second."

The hair stood up on Riq's arms. "One of them is today?"

Kisa nodded.

Riq powered down the SQuare and stuck it back in his satchel, looking all around the battered hut, trying to think. He saw old cooking tools and fallen boards and cloth. He saw a half-covered piece of wood that had been carved into a snake head. Riq knew he needed to tell Sera about the significance of today as soon as he possibly could. The Hystorians really had led them here intentionally. It was now just a matter of figuring out why. Dozens of images flashed through his mind: Itchik leading them into his hut; the scribes coming up out of the rubble; the storm as seen from the mouth of the cave; Jasaw burning incense over Dak's lifeless body.

"Is everything okay?" Kisa asked.

"I'm not sure," Riq said. "I just know I need to get to Sera. You've helped us tremendously, Kisa. And please—"

"Don't worry," Kisa said, cutting him off. "I will not mention the riddle to a soul."

Riq nodded. "Thank you."

"Be careful, Riq. I don't want anything to happen to you."

Riq squeezed her hand and turned to leave, but he only made it as far as the open door before spinning back around. "I need to tell you something, Kisa. Something I've been thinking about all day."

"What?"

"The three of us. Me, Dak, and Sera. We've been traveling from place to place, trying to make the world better. It's a quest I prepared for my whole life. But I've realized something since we arrived at your village."

Kisa held the ceiling board, waiting for Riq to finish.

"Maybe helping the entire world is less important than helping a specific community. Because with a community you can see faces. You can know them, and they can know you back." Riq returned to Kisa, took the board out of her hands, and studied it for a few seconds.

"Who lived in this hut before the storm hit?" he asked.

Kisa lowered her eyes. "Me and my family."

Riq nodded. "You know, all my life I've cared more about a quest than I have about people. I believed having a friend would take my focus away from what was important. But I was wrong about that, Kisa. Having a friend is the most important thing in the world."

"It's the most important thing for you, too?" Kisa asked.

"From this day forward."

"And are we friends?"

Riq nodded. "I'd like to think we are. Even though we haven't known each other very long." He handed the board back to Kisa. "Do you think it'd be okay if I stayed here and helped your village rebuild? It would be a great honor if your people would allow me to help."

"We'd like that very much," Kisa said, dropping the board and taking his hands in hers. "I only wish I could do something for you in return. Something just as important."

"You already have," Riq told her.

His heart was racing. But at least the matter was settled. He would stay here and help Kisa and her family. Dak and Sera would be fine without him. They were the important time travelers. And when their mission was successful, Riq's life back home wouldn't be the same. If he even *had* a life there. Here, at least, he would serve a purpose. He would help rebuild a village. And he would be Kisa's friend. And maybe he could even assist the scribes when they started their next project.

"I have to go," Riq said. "Sera needs to know what you've told me."

"And I have to help Mother with the children," Kisa said.

Riq let go of Kisa's hands and started through the door when Kisa called out, "And, Riq."

He turned around.

"Please be careful of those men. I don't want anything to happen to you."

"Nothing can happen to me now, Kisa." Riq left the hut and started running through the village, toward the ball courts. His legs and chest felt incredibly strong, like he could run forever. Like nothing in the world could slow him down.

8

The Significance of Today

SERA SAT in awe as Pacal opened the codex like an accordion and pointed to the top right section. "Here we show the path of Venus," he said. "We tracked its movement in the sky for many years."

Sera looked at the foreign glyphs. Her translation device did little to help her with archaic written text. But it was an amazing thing to see in person. This was the first written language on the entire continent. And it had an almost otherwordly beauty to it. Each glyph was a miniature work of art.

After Sera had followed Itchik and the children to the ball courts, she had met the four visitors from Calakmul. They were squatty, powerful-looking men with dark brown eyes and bushy brown hair. She also met the three scribes, Cocom, Kan Boar, and Pacal. Itchik invited all the men to a special meal inside the temple, prepared by the best cooks in the village. Sera was all set to head back to the cave and check on Dak when Pacal announced that he would skip dinner and do a little more work. Sera was shocked when he then turned and asked if she wanted to accompany him.

She jumped on the offer, thinking she might get a chance to see the codex up close.

"Past generations have followed the movements of the sun and moon and stars." Pacal went on, "And in our first very amateur codex, we did the same thing. But in this much wiser version I believe we are the first to have charted the course of Venus."

"Wait," Sera said, "there's another codex?"

"A very poor one. A learning experience, you might say—though that alone took us years. We call it our trial codex. I wanted it destroyed, but King Itchik insisted he keep it for reasons of nostalgia."

She looked at Pacal, a short old man with bad teeth. There was something very familiar about him. Every time their eyes met she had a strange déjà vu feeling, not a Remnant exactly, but close.

"How'd you see Venus without a telescope?" Sera said.

"Telescope?" Pacal asked. "What is that?"

"Uh, never mind." Sera chided herself in her head. Of course he wouldn't know what a telescope was. "Don't mind me. I tend to make up words when I'm tired."

Pacal stared deep into her eyes, and Sera felt herself tumbling toward that déjà vu feeling again. Only this time she saw the face of a man from her past. A man she hadn't thought about in years. She had been three years old, playing in the yard at her uncle's place, when a large van pulled up. Several men got out, and the leader walked onto the property and talked to Sera's uncle. They had a long, spirited conversation and then the man walked over to Sera; he'd smiled big and knelt down so he could stare deep into her eyes. He was an older man with long gray hair tied back into a braid and a dark leathery face — the kind you might see at the top of a totem pole.

He'd rubbed his chin, still smiling, and said, "You're going to be special, Sera. I can see it in your eyes. But you must understand, there is always a price to pay for being special. You must have strong shoulders. Do you have strong shoulders, Sera?"

She'd nodded but didn't say a word.

He'd stood up and said, "Good." Then he left in the van with the other men.

When Sera's uncle came over to her, he'd said, "You see how rude he is? He didn't even introduce himself."

"Who was he?" Sera had asked, looking up at her uncle.

"Your grandfather," he'd told her.

That was exactly who Pacal reminded her of. The man who said she would be special. Her grandfather.

Sera pulled herself out of her memory and asked Pacal, "So, why is Venus such a big deal anyway?"

Pacal picked up his fine-tipped brush and began painting a ceiba tree on the last panel. "We have learned much from Venus," he said. "This planet tells us when it's best to plant each crop and when we need to prepare for battle."

Sera tried to decide what she thought of basing real-life decisions on the path of a planet. It reminded her of kids at school who always wanted to know what sign of the horoscope everyone was. Sera had never understood that superstitious approach to life. She'd always been about hard science. But Pacal still seemed smart.

"And this section here describes the work we've done with the calendar," Pacal said, pointing to the fifth panel. "Using the Long Count system, we've calculated the dates far into the future."

Sera wished she could explain all the amazing things that happened from Pacal's time up to the modern day. He seemed like the kind of person who would want to hear about everything. But she couldn't go down that road. She had to keep the conversation on the calendar. "So, at any point does your codex mention a curse?"

"A curse?"

"Yeah," Sera said. "A curse that says we're headed toward a Cataclysm and the only people who can save us are the SQ?"

"There is no curse in our codex," Pacal said.

Sera tried another approach. "So, what happens when you get to the last date of your calendar? Will the world come to an end?"

"Oh, no," Pacal said, laughing now. "That will only

mark the end of a cycle. A new cycle will begin immediately after. We hope it is a time of even greater learning."

They talked about other knowledge the scribes had shared in the codex, and something slowly happened in Sera's brain. She stopped listening quite as intently and started thinking about the error messages on the Infinity Ring again. She still had no idea what the date was. But the Maya kept track of time by another system. And it was an extremely detailed system based on decades of scientific observation and record keeping. That meant raw data, which she could cross-reference with the data stored in the Ring.

Sera slipped the Ring out of her satchel and stared at it. Pacal continued to paint the ceiba tree. At one point he looked up at the Ring and furrowed his brow, but instead of asking any questions he went back to his codex.

After a few minutes, he cleared his throat and said, "Can I offer a word of advice, Sera?"

"I'm all ears," she answered.

"I've come to believe that everything is of this earth. Including you and me. The most complex human invention already existed in the soil. We do not make up new things out of thin air; we simply find already existing elements, born of this earth, and place them in new combinations. Progress is merely organization and creativity."

Sera nodded, trying to process what she'd just heard.

Pacal put down his paintbrush and reached into his

bag. He turned his back on her. "And one other thing," he said. "Never forget the importance of laughter." He turned back around wearing a wooden clown mask, stuck his thumbs in his ears, and wiggled his fingers. "I usually only pull this out when I want to entertain small children."

Sera definitely wasn't expecting this. "So, wait . . . I'm like a small child to you?"

"The best part of all of us is a child," he said.

Sera cracked up a little. It was funny to see the village wise man goofing around with a silly mask.

A few seconds later an alarm went off in her head.

The clown reference in the riddle. Maybe they'd already found the snake charmer *and* the clown. Before Sera could fire off all her questions for Pacal, though, Itchik pushed open the temple doors and led the four visitors from Calakmul into the room, saying, "And here, my friends, is the surprise I told you about." He pointed at the codex. "Our greatest achievement of learning."

The four men stood there nodding and staring at the codex as Pacal pulled off his clown mask and shoved it back in his bag.

Itchik guided the visitors deeper into the temple, saying, "Pacal will describe for you all that our codex explains."

Sera saw that one of the men was looking at the Ring in front of her. She couldn't worry about that now, though. She was too busy reviewing all their previous coordinates. There was astronomical data there, which she cross-referenced with the codex's detailed information on Venus and the moon. She was able to deduce a likely date: July 25, 638. Her hypothesis was confirmed when she reprogrammed the Ring settings and the error messages disappeared.

She pumped her fist and shoved the Ring back into her satchel and stood up.

Pacal was now leading the four visitors through each panel. A second group of people shuffled into the temple as Pacal explained the calendar. A few locals. The other two scribes. "Sera," someone said. She saw Riq step into view and wave her over to him.

As Pacal continued, Sera slipped around the visitors to get to Riq. "I'm so happy you showed up," she said. "I have major news."

"Me, too," he said. "I just spoke to Kisa. She helped me understand the numerical part of the riddle. Apparently, there are two dates listed."

"And?"

Riq seemed more excited than she'd ever seen him. "Sera, one of those dates is today."

"Today?" Sera repeated.

"See? We were supposed to come here all along. Just like I thought. All we have to do now is figure out what's significant about today."

Pacal was now speaking about the path of Venus.

"That's huge," Sera said. "Speaking of the riddle, you'll never guess what that Pacal guy just pulled onto his face a few minutes before you got here."

"What?"

"A clown mask," Sera said. "He has to be the clown from the riddle."

Riq's eyes grew big. "We're finally figuring this thing out," he said.

Sera nodded and said, "Which makes me think Kisa really is the snake charmer. We just need to figure out what that means, exactly. But here's the best news of all." She patted the satchel holding the Infinity Ring and said, "You're looking at the girl who just figured out how to eliminate all those error messages."

"Are you serious?"

Sera explained how Pacal's description of the Mayan calendar helped her figure it out. "The point is," she said, shoving Riq in the shoulder, "we can now leave whenever we want."

"That's . . ." Riq suddenly looked concerned. "I mean, great work, Sera."

"What's wrong?" she asked.

"What? Nothing."

"Are you sure?"

Riq nodded. "Of course I'm sure. But we should probably concentrate on the significance of today's date for now, right?"

"Definitely," Sera said. She turned when she noticed

two of the visitors heading for the door. One of them glanced at her before stepping outside the temple.

Sera held a finger up to Riq and moved toward the group of Mayas listening to Pacal. "Where did they go?" she asked Cocom.

"To meet up with the rest of their men," he answered. "They said the storm set them back and they need to make it to the next village by morning."

"They're not even staying the night?" Sera mumbled to herself as she moved back toward Riq. "That seems sort of weird."

It was twenty more minutes before Pacal finished explaining the final panel of the codex. The two remaining visitors were beyond impressed. They raved to Itchik, who had a big smile on his face, and they patted Pacal on the shoulder and then the smaller of them began folding up the codex, saying, "Yuknoom the Great will be honored to display this in the very center of our empire."

Itchik's smile quickly faded. "We can't let the codex leave Izamal, of course. But King Yuknoom is welcome to send his own scribes here to make a reproduction."

"Oh, no," one of the visitors said, "the king was very specific about this. We are to bring back all of the great achievements we encounter on our journey."

Itchik glanced at his own men behind him. "I'm sorry, friends," he said, moving forward. "I cannot allow —"

"Stay where you are," the larger of the two visitors said, pulling a large obsidian blade from a pouch on his belt and holding it out toward Itchik. "I will make this simple. We are taking the codex back to Calakmul with or without your consent."

Sera and Riq looked at each other, wide-eyed.

The man pulled Pacal toward him and put the knife to his neck. "You don't want us to harm the wise old man, do you? Understand, I have over two dozen men out there waiting for us. If anyone follows us there will be terrible consequences, including the loss of one of your own."

All the local men, including Itchik, stepped back as the two visitors exited the temple, shoving Pacal to the floor. As soon as they were gone, everyone spoke at once, and Sera couldn't understand a thing. She went over and helped Pacal to his feet.

"Silence!" Itchik shouted.

The room went quiet.

"We are not going to let anyone take our codex," Itchik began. "And more important, nobody touches our precious Pacal. Now we need to organize a large group to go after these men. Cocom, go alert the warriors and have the cooks prepare several days' worth of rations. Kan Boar, I need you to prepare a map with all the possible routes to Calakmul. A few of us will follow them now — because I'm not so sure about the extra men they claim to have — and others will cut them off from the front. Men, we will not return without our codex."

Riq turned to Sera and said, "I'm going with them."

"It's not a good idea," Sera said. "You said yourself, we need to stick together."

"I know, Sera. But I have to help them right now. This may be the very reason we're here."

She nodded. "I'll go check on Dak. I want us to be prepared to leave immediately."

Sera watched Riq join the small group of Mayan men who were about to go after the visitors who had taken the codex. One of the men handed Riq a crude version of a sword. Riq turned and met eyes with Sera, and then turned back to the man giving instructions. Sera could tell something had changed in Riq. She just didn't know what it was.

She slipped out the door and started toward the cave.

It was still light out but the sun was low on the horizon. She moved out of the village and began climbing the path up to the cave when a man suddenly stepped out in front of her. It was one of the visitors who had left the temple early, the one who had stared at the Infinity Ring.

Sera instinctively turned to run the other way, but she ran right into the arms of the other visitor who had left early. He spun her around to face the first man, who said, "We came here because we heard rumors about the wisdom of the local codex. But we will leave with more than that." He pointed at Sera's satchel and said, "Remove the device from the bag."

"What device?" Sera said, trying to wiggle her way out of the other man's grasp.

"You know the one I'm speaking of," he said, moving toward her. "Remove the device, and show me what it does."

The Comeback Kid

DAK HAD been dreaming for what seemed like days, and it was all one continuous dream. He had fallen into the deep well by his parents' house, and now he was slowly trying to climb out. But he could only climb a step at a time, because he had to dig out each new handhold into the soft rock with a set of keys. He'd dig for hours and hours with the sharpest key, one of the keys that opened his parents' secret lab, and then he'd test the carved-out gap with his fingers. If it were deep enough to get a good grip, he would pull himself up, shoving his foot into one of the holes he'd previously dug.

Every once in a while there would be a voice above him. He couldn't see because the sky was pitch black, but he didn't need to see to know whose voice it was. He'd been listening to Sera blabber all his life. She spoke to him about their mission and her worries, but she also read him the Mayan riddle, over and over, to the point that he now had it memorized.

But something was changing about his dream now. He was no longer digging handholds with the lab keys; he was using the key his parents had given him when he'd seen them in 911 France. And the hole above him was growing lighter, like morning was taking over the sky above the well. And the voice calling to him was no longer Sera but someone else. A different girl. And soon Dak found himself right up near the top of the well, and this new-girl-who-wasn't-Sera reached for his hand and lifted him up into the light until he fell over the lip of the well and opened his eyes, shouting, "I've got it! I've figured out the riddle!"

"What?" the girl said.

He was startled to find himself not on the ground beside a well but in a dingy cave with the faces of two strangers hovering above him. One of the faces, the female one, belonged to a girl he remembered from the Mayan hut that crumbled in the storm — he winced as the memory of the falling wall flashed through his head. The other face belonged to an old wrinkly dude who had a bunch of feathers sticking up around his dome.

"Dak?" the girl said. "Can you hear me?"

Dak sprang up to a sitting position and looked around. He was behind a hanging blanket surrounded by dozens of flower bouquets and plates of food. "Where am I?" he demanded.

"You're awake," the girl said. Then she turned to the feather dude and shouted, "He's awake!"

"You should remain lying down," the man told Dak.

But Dak wasn't in a lying-down kind of mood. "Where's Sera?" he demanded. "And Riq? What'd you do with my friends?"

"They're both down in the village," the girl said. "You were knocked unconscious in my uncle's hut. People carried you here so you could rest and our healer could take care of you." She pointed at the man next to her. "This is Jasaw. And I'm Kisa."

Dak rubbed his eyes and looked all around, the back of his head throbbing.

"And do you see all these gifts around you?" the girl asked him.

"Tough to miss," Dak said, stretching out his stiff neck.

"They're from the people of my village. If it weren't for you, I don't know what would have happened to my cousin."

"No need to toss roses," Dak told her, his thoughts finally clearing. "That's just sort of what I do, Kisa."

"What do you mean?"

"I save lives."

The girl didn't even crack a smile. "Well, we are all very much in your debt."

Dak shrugged and reached down for what looked like a hunk of good ol' American cheese, but as soon as he took a bite he realized it was squash and spit it back onto the plate, cursing himself because America hadn't even been founded yet, so how could there be American cheese? He wiped his mouth on his bare arm and motioned toward the healer. "This dude doesn't have a whole lot to say." The man was putting herbs into little wooden boxes.

"He's been busy because of the storm. Several people were injured." Kisa moved closer and looked right into Dak's eyes. She turned to the healer and said, "Do you think he's okay to walk down to the village?"

"Not a good idea, but the boy is free to do what he thinks he can."

Kisa turned back to Dak and said, "I'm sorry to weigh you down with troubles when you're just now feeling better—"

"But . . . ?"

"But I kind of need your help. I'm worried about your friends, actually."

Dak felt a surge of energy and stood up. "Something happened to Sera?"

"Well, I'm not sure yet," Kisa said. "I'm just worried because—"

"Let's stop wasting time," he interrupted. "We need to go find her. Now!"

"Are you sure you're well enough to walk?" she said.

"Of course I'm sure," he told her. "I could run a marathon if I needed to. Or lift a car. Or jump over a malaria-infested stream." He jumped up and down a few times to prove himself. "See?"

Dak promptly fainted into Kisa's arms.

As they left the cave, Dak's arm wrapped around Kisa's shoulder for support, Kisa said, "When you woke up you said something about solving a riddle. What did you mean by that?"

"Have you ever heard of the Hystorians?" Dak asked.

"Only from you and Riq."

"Have you ever heard of a Time Warden?"

Kisa shook her head.

"That's because they don't exist here yet. Neither group has infiltrated the Americas in this era. That's my theory, at least."

"What are the Americas?" Kisa asked.

Dak took his arm from around Kisa's shoulder. "I'm feeling better," he said. "I think I can make it on my own." He stretched his neck again and reached back to feel the lump on the back of his head. "Anyway, the specifics are not important. The main thing is the question of why we've been sent here. That's what I've figured out."

"And?"

"We're here to protect your codex. To ensure that it is not destroyed by the Spanish conquistadores who are eventually going to invade your land and try to convert you to their own ideologies. It's Censorship 101, Kisa.

Control the masses by controlling the acquisition of information. Your codex is the 'treasure that never was.'"

"I'm not understanding many of the things you're saying."

"It's not important, my fair lady. The point is, there are no Hystorians in Mayan territory, therefore there's no one here to properly secure the codex—which I believe is a very important document. Enter myself, Sera, and Riq."

"There needs to be Hystorians here, then," Kisa said.

"Preaching to the choir, my friend. Preaching to the choir."

"But this is exactly why I came for you, Dak. Some men showed up in the village today, and Itchik—"

"My man, Itchy," Dak interrupted. "How is that guy? He never calls. He never writes."

"He's well," Kisa said, flustered. "Itchik believes they only want to study the codex, but I'm afraid they have come here to take it for their own. The people from Calakmul believe they have a right to anything they want."

Dak stopped and turned to Kisa. "Trust me, we're not gonna let that happen."

"Good," she said.

They walked halfway down the lush, tropical path before Dak heard voices. He stopped again and held Kisa back by the arm. He put a finger to his lips as a sign for her to keep quiet, and then he crept up the path a few more paces until he had an obscured view of a short squatty man who kept peeking back over his shoulder, like he was acting as a lookout man. Dak crept up a little closer, and he saw the heads of two others in the bushes. A man and a girl with brown hair . . .

Dak's heart climbed up into his throat.

The man was holding a knife to the girl's throat, and the girl was Sera.

And the lookout man was holding the Infinity Ring. It was like a great big déjà vu moment. Last time he had sprinted at the pack and tackled the man holding the Ring. And it had been a mistake. But as Dak sat there, studying the scene, he realized something: He would always race to help Sera when she appeared to be in danger. He didn't care how many times it was a mistake. There was no way he would ever be able to just sit back and let something possibly happen to her. No way. Not on his watch.

He stood up, still a bit wobbly on his feet, and then he sprinted at the man holding the Infinity Ring, just like he had a few days earlier, yelling, "Nobody messes with my friends!" Only this time he sidestepped that man at the last second and plowed into the man holding a knife to Sera's throat. The knife went flying, and so did Dak and the man.

"Dak!" Sera shouted.

"Dak!" Kisa shouted.

Dak and the man both tumbled into the jungle brush,

and the back of Dak's already wounded head smacked into a tree.

He was dazed.

The whole jungle swirled around him.

He could hear details of sound he'd never heard before: the whining of mosquitoes and the hot wind rustling the leaves of every tree in the jungle and the songs of faraway birds and the cracking of twigs as he scrambled back to his feet without even telling himself to scramble back to his feet. He found himself face-to-face with the man he'd just knocked over.

The man was grinning. "Glad you could join us," he said.

Over the man's shoulders Dak saw Sera and Kisa trying to wrestle the other guy to the ground. The Infinity Ring lay in the grass near their feet.

He lunged for the man again, but the Maya stepped to the side and threw Dak to the ground. He looked up at the man, who was still grinning, knowing Dak was no match, especially in his current physical condition. And Dak saw that the other dude now had Sera and Kisa pinned to the ground, a firm grip on each of their necks.

It was over.

The man in front of Dak stepped on Dak's back and told his friend, "Release the younger girl," he said.

The man did, and Sera stood up, looking very hesitant. "Dak," she said. "You're okay."

"Well, technically not at the moment," he said, pointing up at the man standing on him. "But, yeah, I'm no longer bedridden. What's going on here?"

"I'll tell you what's going on," the man above him said. "We came here to retrieve a local codex, but we've stumbled into something potentially even greater. This metal thing your friend has."

"Our king, Yuknoom the Great, will be very happy," the other man said.

"He'll be even more satisfied when we understand how to use it." The man standing on Dak reached down for his obsidian knife. He dug a knee into Dak's back and held the knife to his neck. "So we're clear about things," he said to Sera, "you're going to explain how the item works, or I'm going to slice your little friend into several pieces."

"Easy with all that 'little' talk," Dak said. "Besides, the item in question no longer even works. Tell him how I broke it, Sera."

Sera shot him an uneasy look.

"Wait, you fixed it?" Dak said.

"Sort of."

"How could you?!"

"Quiet!" the man kneeling on Dak said. "If you continue talking, I'll slice you up just to get some peace and quiet. Now, go on." He motioned for Sera to pick up the Ring.

Sera slowly reached down, pulled the Ring off the grass.

"First of all," the man continued, "what is it?"

Lie to him, Dak thought. *Make something up. Tell him it's a can opener.*

"It's a time-traveling device," Sera said.

Dak let his face fall into the grass.

"It allows you to warp to whatever era you program into it," Sera went on. "We are from the future."

The man holding down Dak looked at his friend and said, "Are you hearing this? We will be legends in Calakmul!"

"Yuknoom will build temples in our honor," the man replied.

Dak lifted his head. Sera was holding the Ring out for the men to see. Kisa was squeezing her eyes shut, like she was injured.

"How do you go to another time?" the man above Dak asked.

"It's simple," Sera said. "You just program in —"

"Uh, Sera?" Dak interrupted. "Maybe a little less detail here?"

"As I was saying," Sera said, keeping her eyes on the man, "you just program in your desired year and geographic location, and the machine will take you there. But there's a catch."

"And what is that?"

"The machine will not work unless the three of us" — she gestured to herself, Dak, and Kisa — "are in physical contact with it. It is programmed to respond only to our DNA."

The squat man looked at his friend. "What is DNA?"

Kisa began humming in a strange way, like it was helping her manage the pain. And her eyes were still squeezed shut.

The other guy shrugged. "Who cares? Let's just take the machine and let the king worry about it from there."

"DNA," Sera said, "is a nucleic acid that contains the specific genetic code of each unique organism. In other words, it's a way to decipher that you are you and I am me. No two people have the same DNA. And the machine, as I've already explained, will only work if it is in direct contact with the DNA of all three of us."

"The girl is deranged," the squat man said.

"Oh, I disagree," the man above Dak said. "In fact, she's given me an idea. If this thing needs something from each of them in order to work, then we simply cut off a hand from all three of them. We will bring back to Calakmul the codex, this machine, and three hands."

"It's genius," the other man said.

Dak's captor brought his obsidian knife down to Dak's wrist. He began a sawing motion. Dak screamed.

"Dak!" Sera shouted.

But the man kept sawing, and Dak was pinned in such an awkward position he couldn't even move.

And then suddenly the man began shouting, "No! Please!" And he let go of Dak and hopped off him. The other man was shouting, too.

Dak twisted around to see what was going on. He spotted a few large snakes slithering out of the dense jungle foliage. Their tongues whipped around outside of their mouths and then sucked back in.

Dak and Sera both started screaming, too.

Kisa just lay there, cringing in pain.

But an odd thing happened. The snakes slithered right over Kisa. They appeared to be converging on the two Mayan men, ignoring the kids entirely.

"It's witchcraft!" cried the man with the knife.

"Run!" yelled the other.

As soon as the men had disappeared into the trees, the snakes dispersed. It was hard to tell whether they were in pursuit or simply passing through.

Dak staggered to his feet, holding his wrist. "What just happened?"

Sera pointed to Kisa, who was now sitting up. "Did she just save our lives?"

Dak looked at Kisa, who was fingering the locket around her neck. "Sometimes I come out here when I'm bored, and I hum to them. But nothing like this ever happened."

Dak turned to Sera. "Dude, she's like one of those

guys who plays the flute or whatever and gets a snake to dance around."

"Maybe, said Sera. "Maybe they were just . . . migrating. Do snakes migrate?"

"You have to go find Riq now," Kisa said.

"What about you?" Dak said.

"I need to be alone for a few minutes. I will be right behind you."

Dak turned to Sera and shrugged.

"Come on," said Sera. "I think I know which way Riq was headed."

Hand Over That Thief

"Quiet, men," Itchik said, his chest heaving in and out. "It won't be long now."

But Riq noted that the king of Izamal was breathing just as loudly as the rest of them. They'd run several miles through the hot and humid jungle — taking the "long road" out of town, as Itchik called it. Sweat streamed down Riq's face, stinging his eyes, salting his lips. But he tried to follow orders and breathe more quietly.

The plan was to take a different route than the men from Calakmul, circling around to cut them off from the front. Once they saw the men emerge on the path, Riq would spring into action. His particular role in Itchik's plan was by far the most dangerous, but he wasn't complaining. This was his purpose now. To help the people of Kisa's village. And if helping them meant putting his life at risk, that's exactly what he'd do.

"Easy, men," Itchik said, regaining his breath.

As they waited, Riq thought about how different his new life would be. A few days ago he was a thousand percent committed to the Hystorian mission. It was the very blood that pumped through his veins . . . and always would. But today he was going to step away from the front lines of the Hystorians' struggle. His loyalty now belonged to the people of Izamal. And Kisa. His heart hammered inside his chest as he imagined waking up in this jungle village for the rest of his days.

Itchik turned to Riq, said, "You ready, son?"

"I'm ready, sir," Riq said.

"Remember, just toss the codex over your shoulder when you get it. Huracan will be there to pick it up."

"Yes, sir." Riq glanced back at Huracan. The man nodded to him. Then Riq glanced at the man who had possession of the trial codex. It was inside a leather bag slung across his shoulder.

Riq whipped his head back around when he heard hushed voices coming from the path. Men from Calakmul were approaching. He raised up into a squat, readying himself to scamper through the dense foliage and onto the footpath, but Itchik held Riq by the elbow and shook his head. "Not yet," he mouthed, pointing toward the path.

Riq saw that there were six men walking in a tight formation. But none of them had been in the temple with Pacal. And there was no sign of the codex.

"They were telling the truth," Itchik whispered back

to his men. "They have reinforcements."

After the men had passed, Itchik continued, "I've seen this tactic before. They have a group of men lead the way, scouting the path. Then we will see a middle group, which will likely include the men who took the codex. And finally, there will be a scout group bringing up the rear. We will have to act quickly, men. Our plan will have to be fully executed before the final group is upon us."

Riq expected to see the second group right away, but there was more waiting. And the longer he waited, the more questions came into his head. What if he couldn't wrestle the codex away from whomever was carrying it? What if he failed in his very first role as a member of Kisa's community? Or what if the men who'd stolen the codex went a completely different way? He wiped sweat from his forehead and swallowed. If there really was going to be a second group, what was taking them so long?

Seconds later, he heard the cracking of branches in the jungle behind him and spun around. The rest of the men turned around, too, some brandishing their knives. To Riq's complete surprise, it was Sera who emerged . . . with Dak! One of the warriors put a finger to his lips, urging them to keep quiet.

But Dak snuck over to Riq anyway and knelt beside him. "You have to come with us," he whispered.

"You're walking around again?" Riq said.

"I'm more than just walking around." Dak stood up

and did a stupid five-second dance, then knelt back down. "Seriously, though, you need to come with us."

"Can't do it," Riq said.

Sera leaned over their shoulders, whispering in Spanish so that their translators would have to recalibrate, allowing them a moment of privacy within the crowd. "We've figured out the riddle, Riq. We're supposed to take the codex with us. And I was able to work out the second date from the riddle. It's in 1562! That must be our next stop."

Riq balked. "Why would you take the codex with you?"

Itchik shot them both a look. Riq knew he couldn't understand what they were saying, but he wanted them to be silent.

"Uh, to protect it?" Dak whispered. "Sera told me some guys already tried to steal it. We both believe this is the Break we're supposed to fix before we move on. And we seriously need to move on."

Riq looked over his shoulder at Sera, who was nodding. He turned back to Dak, who whispered, "Come on, dude, be a team player."

"If you don't quit bothering me," Riq whispered back, "we'll never get the codex back. We're waiting for the people who have it to pass. Now go on. Shoo."

"I see," Dak said, rubbing his hands together. "Finally, a bit of that Mayan warmongering I've been hoping for."

Riq shook his head. The kid was much easier to get

along with when he was unconscious.

"Look," Dak whispered, "one of us has to grab it so we can warp the heck out of this place. Sera has the Ring all programmed and ready to go. Here's an idea: Let's live to fix another Break. This place has been hard on my system."

Riq stared at Dak, trying to decide the best way to break the news that he wasn't going anywhere. Because it was definitely best to get that part out of the way. "I wanted to talk to you about that, Dak," he began. "I've been doing a lot of thinking over the last couple days—"

"Well, there's a step in the right direction," Dak said.

"Ha-ha. Anyway I'm just going to come out and say it. I'm not going to continue on from—" Riq wasn't able to finish his sentence because right then Itchik grabbed his elbow again and pointed down at the path.

Riq turned and saw five men walking up the hill—including the two he'd seen in the temple earlier. One of them had the folded-up codex tucked under his left arm.

Riq furiously waved Dak away.

This was his moment.

Itchik held on to Riq's elbow until the last possible second, then he pushed Riq out from behind the trees. Riq's adrenaline kicked in as he scampered down the densely packed hill, shouting at the Calakmul men, "Take me with you! Please! They'll kill me!"

The men stopped, clearly caught off guard.

The front three pulled their knives.

Itchik and a few of his warriors followed Riq down the hill, commanding, "Stop that boy! He is to be punished for his crimes!"

Riq pushed past the first row of Calakmul men and jumped onto the man holding the codex. "Please!" he continued shouting. "They'll kill me!"

"Get off him!" the men with knives shouted. One slashed Riq's cheek, blood instantly trickling down his face and neck. But Riq kept his wits about him. He had to execute the plan. He yanked the codex out of the man's hands, still pleading for help, and tossed it over his shoulder.

Riq glanced back in time to see Huracan pick it up and pretend to hand it to Itchik, who already had the trial codex in his possession. Itchik then thrust the trial codex up over his head and shouted, "Men, this belongs to you! Take back your codex and display it in the greatest empire in all the land! All I ask in return is that you hand over that thief!"

The Calakmul men were busy kicking at Riq and slugging him in the back and head. Riq covered himself and closed his eyes, and he could now hear Dak and Sera screaming for the men to stop, but the beating didn't stop until Itchik stepped over Riq and waved everyone away. He handed over the trial codex, and pulled Riq to his feet . . . only to slug him square in the jaw.

Riq was facedown on the path again with no memory of falling.

"Take him!" Itchik shouted back at his warriors.

Several of Itchik's men picked Riq up and held his arms behind his back as Itchik announced, "This boy was caught looting huts in the wake of the great storm! He will be punished in the square!"

Riq was slightly dazed from all the abuse he'd taken, but he was still clearheaded enough to smile on the inside. The plan was working perfectly. The Calakmul men had backed off. Huracan had already left for the village to hide the real codex. The man holding the fake looked through a few pages of glyphs, but didn't seem to have any clue that there was a difference.

Itchik commanded to his men, "Lead him back! Now!"

But before they could take Riq anywhere, one of the Calakmul men said, "Why not sacrifice him right here in the jungle? Isn't that what a thief deserves?"

"Yeah, do him in now!" another shouted. "So we can watch!"

"No!" a voice from the crowd yelled.

Riq looked up to see Kisa hurrying through the foliage and onto the path.

"He didn't steal anything!" she shouted, shoving one of the men who held Riq. The man laughed, managing to keep ahold of Riq.

"It's okay," Riq said to Kisa under his breath.

Kisa ignored Riq and shouted at Itchik. "He didn't steal anything! It's all a bunch of lies!"

Many of the Calakmul men were laughing now. Which meant, Riq realized, they were no longer calling for his head. Itchik played along with Kisa's assertion by commanding, "We will attend to this matter back in the village. A verdict on the thief will be made by this evening so the gods can bear witness." Then he turned to the visitors from Calakmul and said, "Men, I thank you for capturing the prisoner. Please give my regards to Yuknoom the Great."

They all nodded. One said, "A couple of our men are missing. If you come across those misfits—"

"You can try them before the gods, too," another man interjected.

All the Calakmul men laughed.

The first man continued, "Tell them we're already on our way to the next village."

"Of course," Itchik said.

Riq couldn't believe his eyes; the men from Calakmul were all turning and continuing down the jungle path, away from Izamal. The plan had worked. Itchik's men were all quietly congratulating one another as Riq reached up to touch his bloody cheek.

"Kisa," Itchik said, grinning from ear to ear. "How you always innately sense what's happening, I'll never understand."

"You knew it was all part of the plan?" Riq asked.

Kisa nodded. "I knew Itchik would never strike an unarmed person. It had to be an act." Riq saw that she was holding a metal locket with a chain.

"Yes, I'm very sorry about the punch," Itchik said. "You've sacrificed so much for us, son."

Riq felt a rush of pride as he watched Itchik join his men, but there was a worried look on Kisa's face. "What's wrong?" he asked her.

"You will not stay here," she said.

"What do you mean?" Riq said. "I thought it was all settled."

"I've changed my mind. I want you to go."

Riq's whole body felt suddenly paralyzed. "I don't understand," he said. "Earlier you said—"

"It only matters what I'm saying now," she said with a stern look on her face. "Please go, Riq."

Dak and Sera pushed through the men to get to him. "Wow," Dak said. "You took some serious abuse."

"Are you okay?" Sera asked. "We tried to rush down here to help, but the men hiding in the bushes stopped us and told us all about the plan. You agreed to this?"

Riq nodded, but he could hardly follow Sera's words. He was too numb from what Kisa had just said to him. He watched her back away, wondering what had changed. Why was she so against him staying now?

"We're leaving right this second," Dak said. "We heard there might be another group coming through here, and I don't want to take any chances."

Sera was already kneeling down onto the path and reaching into her satchel for the Ring. She pulled it out and powered it on.

Riq looked at Kisa. He decided he had to stay anyway. She would come around in time. "Dak, Sera," he began, "this is very hard for me to say, but—"

"Do you all have everything you need?" Kisa interrupted, pushing herself forward again.

"I think we do," Dak said. He turned to Riq. "Sera and I now believe the codex is supposed to remain here in the village under Kisa and Pacal's protection. Right, Sera? You think our mission was just to get it back from those men?"

"I'm positive," Sera answered, looking up. "Which we've done thanks to you, Riq."

"Honestly," Dak said. "Great work, dude."

Riq was going to try one more time to explain he intended to stay, but then he saw the callous look on Kisa's face. Like he suddenly disgusted her. And then one of Itchik's men said, "Look!" His finger was pointing down the path to where a third group of Calakmul men was fast approaching. There were at least fifteen men marching in formation, less than fifty yards away.

"Come on!" Dak shouted at Sera. "We need to do this now!"

"I'm trying!" Sera shouted back.

Itchik and his men were already retreating up into the jungle. Riq grabbed Kisa's arm before she could go and said, "You really want me to leave?"

She stared back at him, completely straight-faced, and said simply, "Yes." Then she handed Riq the locket. Riq looked at the snake carved into the front of it. Then he looked up at Kisa, his heart breaking. "But I thought—"

"You thought wrong," she said, cutting him off.

He let her go—the only thing he could do—and watched her disappear into the bushes.

"Stay where you are!" one of the Calakmul men shouted at Riq, Dak, and Sera.

Riq turned and saw the men hurrying toward them.

"Now, Sera!" Dak shouted.

"Got it!" she shouted back. "Grab on!"

Riq reluctantly reached for a part of the Ring, staring up at the tree Kisa had just ducked behind. His face stung. And his back and ribs and head were pulsing with pain. But that was nothing compared to the pain he felt inside. Something had changed for Kisa. She no longer wanted him around.

The men were less than ten yards away when Sera shouted, "Here we go!"

The Ring brightened, and Riq was so jarred by the abrupt feeling of its power that he accidentally dropped the locket onto the ground. "Wait!" he shouted, reaching down for it, but just before he could wrap his fingers around the snake's metal tail he was whisked away into blackness and it was lost.

11

What Sera Saw

SERA IS sucked right back into her memory of the Cataclysm.

She sees herself in the small motorized emergency raft again, speeding through intersection after intersection. And she's screaming, begging for all of it to stop. The fires. The flooding. The acid rain pouring down from above. The earth's violent shaking.

Sera zips past several miles of absolute destruction until she's out of the city and turns onto her childhood street. She lets off the gas as she nears her house, then dives overboard and swim-walks her way up the flooded driveway. When she reaches a trembling hand out for the doorknob, she half expects to black out or be whisked away—like every other time she's tried to access her memory of the Cataclysm.

But this time she remains present.

She watches herself slowly turn the knob, push open the door, creep inside the only home she's ever known. "Uncle Diego!" she calls out.

No answer.

Sera moves through the living room, leaving the front door wide open behind her. The wood floors are covered in two feet of grayish water. Many of her uncle's possessions are submerged or floating randomly: books, documents, framed photos, candles, old newspapers and magazines, vases. Most of the furniture is overturned. A leg is missing from the dining room table. The TV is knocked over and punctured. The mirror below the clock is shattered and hanging askew. It looks like someone has ransacked the place, looking for something, but what?

The kitchen is even worse. The fridge is wide open and mostly cleaned out, its door ripped from the hinges. The cupboards are full of broken plates and glasses. Sera stops cold when she sees the empty wooden knife block. The utensil drawer is still full of forks and spoons. But the knives are gone. Where are the knives?

"Uncle Diego!" she calls out again.

Nothing.

Sera sloshes out of the kitchen, but when she rounds the corner she lets out a short scream. There, frozen on the stairs, is a rail-thin man wearing her uncle's raincoat. Long, unkempt hair and shaggy beard. Bugged eyes. The man looks half-dead already.

Sera's heart is beating inside her throat as she says, "Who are you?"

Instead of answering, the man leaps down the rest of

the stairs and splashes his way across the living room.

"Stop!" Sera shouts, but he's already out the door.

She bounds up the waterlogged stairs, her whole body now wired with fear. What if something happened to her uncle? She pushes open her own bedroom door first. A few items are scattered around the floor. But otherwise it's the way she left it. She continues to her uncle's bedroom door and reaches for the doorknob, preparing herself for what she might find.

She slowly pushes open the door and looks around.

There's an unfamiliar sleeping bag in the middle of the room. Trash piled in the far corner. But nothing else out of the ordinary. The man she'd just seen had most likely been living there. But for how long? And where was her uncle?

That's when it hits Sera.

She has to go and see about the barn.

The rushing water is up to Sera's waist as she steps up to the front door of the barn. She has to keep a wide stance and lean against the current to keep from getting swept away. Before she pulls open the heavy door she flashes back to all the Remnants she's had over the years, many of which have involved this very barn. She's always known it's important. But she's afraid to find out why.

Sera forces herself to pull open the door, and as soon

as it's halfway open she peeks her head inside and sees a body floating faceup in the water.

She immediately falls to her knees, sobbing.

Her uncle Diego.

The only family she's ever known.

His face strangely contorted, eyes wide open.

She covers her own face, and then slaps down at the water and stands back up. Behind her uncle she spots four more bodies. All floating facedown.

She moves toward them, hiccupping and gasping for breath, tears streaming down her face. Her right hand shakes as she reaches out for the dead man's cold arm, turns over his body. It's a face she's never seen before. But at the same time, it's oddly familiar. She turns over a dead woman next to him, which evokes the same strange feeling. She can't pinpoint the familiarity. But it's incredibly powerful.

The third and fourth bodies make her fall to her knees again, slapping at the water and shouting, "No! Please!"

Dak's parents.

She buries her face in her hands and cries so hard that strange animal sounds are escaping from her throat and she can hardly breathe.

And then a horrific thought occurs to her and she looks up at the first two bodies again. She stares at their faces. Then she looks at Dak's parents again and back at her uncle. The two unknown faces are oddly familiar. Oddly like her own face.

"No," she whispers, moving back toward the first man again, studying his eyes and mouth. "No."

She reaches into his back pocket for his wallet, then pulls out his ID and reads the name:

Daniel Froste.

Her father.

She stares down at the man without crying or breathing, and then she looks at the woman. Her mother. Then she angles her own face up at the ceiling and screams so piercingly loud her ears continue ringing long after she closes her mouth.

The parents she's never known have come back for her.

And now they're dead.

Sera rips at her own hair and forces her head underwater, right cheek pressed up against the muddy ground. She stays like this until her lungs burn and her thoughts grow thin and disappear, and she can no longer stand the pain in her chest.

Still she refuses to let herself up, and then the memory slips away and she is lost.

1 2

One Thousand Years Later

SERA OPENED her eyes, shaking uncontrollably.

Her body no longer felt real now that she'd broken through her repressed memory of the Cataclysm. She felt fake. Made up. Though she was clearly sitting on the clay dirt, behind a massive building, it felt like she was floating floating floating. Up into the sky. Into nothingness.

Everyone was going to die.

Including the parents she'd always dreamed about. They would die trying to fight their way back to her. She'd find them in her uncle's barn.

Her Remnants would forever take on an entirely different meaning.

Sera turned and saw Dak and Riq looking around, taking in their new environment — which wasn't new so much as updated. They'd landed in the exact same place they'd landed the last time they warped. Mayan country. Izamal. In a large patch of tall, thick grass. Except where the fallen observatory rubble once lay, a beautiful new observatory, twice the size of its predecessor, now stood.

Itchik had done exactly what he had promised. And the temple, where Sera had just watched Pacal paint a ceiba tree into the codex, had been transformed into a massive church.

Judging by the sun, it was late afternoon. The people walking the raised white road in the distance were a combination of traditional Mayas and white men dressed in pious robes. Sera knew right away they were the Franciscan monks she'd read about, the ones who settled in Mayan villages and tried to convert the indigenous people to their own religious beliefs.

"I'm not saying anything this time," Dak suddenly announced.

Sera found Dak staring at her. Poor Dak. Her best friend had no idea what she'd found in her uncle Diego's barn.

"Nope," Dak said, shaking his head. "I refuse to even bring up the fact that tears are literally streaming down your face. Uh-uh. My lips are sealed."

Sera couldn't bring herself to tell him about his parents. It was too awful. And it was way off in the future. At the same time, Dak was so worried about his parents being lost in time. Wouldn't he want to know that they'd made their way back?

Sera stared at Dak, trying to decide if it was better to know the unbearable truth or live as long as possible in happy ignorance.

"Know why I'm keeping quiet?" Dak said. "Because

it's none of my business. Who am I to point out that you're shaking like a hairless dog in the snow?"

"It's just the warp again," Sera managed to say.

Dak held up his hands, saying, "Eh, eh, eh. No need to even discuss it, Sera. I'm steering clear of your hysterics from now on." He turned to Riq, said, "I see Lover Boy over here has the same strategy."

Riq didn't even look up.

"Wow," Dak said, turning back to Sera. "What's wrong with you people? Last time I checked, I was the one who nearly got decapitated by a falling wall."

Sera tried to think up something lighthearted to say back, to at least pretend things were normal, but her mind drew a blank. Every time she looked at Dak she remembered turning over the bodies of his dead parents. And that made her remember the faces of her own dead parents, too. And her uncle Diego.

Dak pulled the SQuare out of Riq's satchel, shaking his head. He turned on the power. "Nobody has a sense of humor anymore," he said, typing something on the keyboard. "What we're doing isn't easy. I understand that. But we have to keep our composure, right? I mean, we have a fairly important job to do." He looked up at Sera. "We have to save the world."

Sera wiped her tearstained face on the arm of her *huipil* and said, "I'm pretty sure we're all aware of that, Dak. Just cut us some slack."

Dak motioned toward Riq with his thumb and

said, "I saw what happened to the Riq-ster over here. His girlfriend or whatever tried to give him a parting gift—a locket or something—but he dropped it. Isn't that right, Riq?"

Sera watched Riq turn to Dak, scowling.

Dak was oblivious, of course. "See, that's why I tell all my bros back home to steer clear of the lovey-dovey stuff. It's asking for trouble, dude. You want my advice? If you absolutely *have* to interact with the opposite sex, make sure it's with a girl you can treat like one of the guys. Like Sera." He kicked at her with one of his feet.

"Wow," Sera said. "That's so . . . sweet of you." Sera might've slugged Dak in the ribs if she hadn't just remembered finding his dead and bloated parents during the Cataclysm.

Riq stood up suddenly. Without saying a word he walked away.

"Hey!" Dak called after him. "You can't leave! It's going to be dark soon! And we're supposed to stick together!"

Riq didn't even turn around.

"Riq!" Sera shouted, but he'd already rounded the corner of the new observatory, out of sight. She turned to Dak. "You happy now?"

"Was it something I said?"

Sera rolled her eyes. "When is it *not* something you said?"

"I was just offering the guy a little romantic guidance." Dak shook his head. "Some people are too sensitive."

"We should go after him," Sera said. She stood up and looked around to try to get her bearings. It was odd seeing all the things that had changed. The updated huts and new trees and paved streets. But at the same time, everything felt so familiar.

"Fine," Dak said. "But first let's look at the latest riddle I just pulled up." Dak turned the SQuare around so Sera could read the screen:

To save the reproduction of the treasure's truth, do the following:
Seek the help of those who follow "the most important thing in the world"
Then dig deep, deeper, deepest, unlocking a long-locked door
It will take a polyglot to understand the wisdom of the glyphs
and the forgery of the curse

Sera read it twice and then she stood back up, shaking her head. "I don't get it."

"Neither do I."

She wasn't surprised the difficulty of the riddles was increasing. She knew that the Hystorians hadn't had time to completely program the SQuare. Things were more vague now. The further they got into the Breaks, the less information they would have.

"What the heck is 'the most important thing in the world'?" Dak said.

Sera shook her head. "No idea."

"It seems like an extension of the first riddle, though," Dak said. "Both talk about truth and the treasure and the curse."

"The 'treasure' is the codex," Sera said. "We know that much."

"And the curse is about the Cataclysm described in the Great Mayan Codex."

Sera just looked at Dak for a few long seconds. "According to Pacal, there was never any mention of a Cataclysm in his codex."

"None?"

Sera shook her head, trying not to think about what *she* knew about the Cataclysm.

"And what does the riddle mean by a 'reproduction'?" Dak asked. "I still wonder if we should've just taken Pacal's codex with us."

Sera was having trouble concentrating now. She'd stare at the words "unlocking a long-locked door" and all of a sudden she'd find herself remembering the Cataclysm again. Her flooded barn. The bodies she had to turn over.

"A *polyglot* has something to do with language, right?" Dak said.

"I'm not sure," Sera said. "But I know someone who would. We really need to go find Riq. We should all be doing this together. And that means you might have to go easy on him for a little while."

"I guess you're right," Dak said, standing up. He looked at Sera. "You know, I really did see him drop a piece of jewelry that Snake Girl had just given him."

Sera had seen the way Riq looked at Kisa. It couldn't have been easy for him to say good-bye. "You missed a few things while you were recovering in the cave," she said.

"I figured as much."

They started walking around the corner of the observatory, in the direction they'd seen Riq go. As soon as they rounded the corner, Sera nearly ran right into a teenage boy. It wasn't Riq, though. It was a Mayan boy who had a large bag slung over his left shoulder. He wore an outfit similiar to Dak's.

"Sorry," he said.

"It's okay," she said, her translator device kicking in to match his dialect.

He straightened his bag and said, "Well, have a nice evening." He started to leave, but then turned around and looked over Sera and Dak for a few seconds, noting their attire, before saying, "A bunch of us are meeting in the cave in a little while. If you're interested in practicing the old ways."

"Maybe we'll join you," Dak said.

Sera and Dak watched the boy hurry along the path that Sera remembered led out of the village and up toward the cave. Dak poked her on the shoulder and said, "A bunch of Mayas racing off to the cave. Isn't this exactly how things started off last time?"

"It is," Sera said, but she had a sneaking suspicion that the cave served a much different function in 1562.

This Is Who We Are

THE WARPING that seemed so hard on everyone else was practically therapeutic for Dak. He couldn't believe how much better he felt as he and Sera continued to wander the village in search of Riq. Only a few days ago — well, a few days ago plus a millennium — a wall had fallen on his head. How many people had had an actual stone wall fall on their head? The number had to be fairly low. And Dak was just walking around like it was nothing. He had to admit, it was a little superhero-esque.

"I'm back, baby," he muttered under his breath.

And being back meant fixing the Breaks, saving the world — all of it hopefully leading to a heartfelt reunion with his parents that would be shown live on some kind of morning news show. And, no, he wouldn't be rocking the breechcloth on national TV.

"I don't see Riq anywhere," Sera said as they moved down a less crowded village path, about a hundred yards from the observatory.

Dak stopped walking and surveyed the scene. The huts were more modern now and slightly larger. And they were packed in more tightly. He turned to Sera. "Dude, we have to start thinking like the guy. Where would you go if you were in love with a charming snake charmer who's been deceased for approximately a millennium?"

Sera shot him a disapproving look.

"What?" Dak said. "I'm trying to put myself in the mind of the missing."

"Not funny." Sera started walking again.

"You have to admit," Dak said, following her. "It was pretty wild what she did with all those snakes."

Sera picked up a rock, tossed it down the path in front of them. "All I know is we were lucky to get out of there alive."

"I'll give you that." Dak watched another small group of Mayas hurry past with bags slung over their shoulders — all of them glancing back down the road behind them, like they were doing something they weren't supposed to. It suddenly occurred to Dak how much these people's lives must have changed since the arrival of the Spanish. One thing was for sure, Dak no longer viewed the Maya as untrustworthy. History hadn't given them nearly enough credit — which made him wonder what else history had gotten wrong.

"What do you think that sculpture symbolizes?" Sera asked, motioning toward the one in front of a stone wall that surrounded a small cluster of huts. It looked like a face partially covered by a net or scales. "I've seen it in a few different places now."

"I've seen it, too," Dak said. "My guess is it reads *In Honor of Dak Smyth, Our Eternal Hero.*"

"Yeah, that's it," Sera scoffed.

"Because of, you know, how I saved that little girl or whatever. You saw all the flowers and food they left me, right?"

Sera rolled her eyes.

Another group of Mayas passed by, slightly larger than the one before. "Excuse me," Sera said to the last young woman. She pointed at the sculpture. "Do you know what that means?"

"Of course," the woman said, backpedaling as she spoke to Sera. "It's the secret symbol of friendship."

"Secret symbol of friendship?" Dak said. "That's weird. If it's so secret, why's it in so many different places?"

The woman looked Dak up and down. It was clear she hadn't noticed him when she'd spoken to Sera. "I'm sorry, but we're actually in a hurry," the woman said. She turned back around and jogged a few steps to catch up with her friends.

Dak looked at Sera. "Clearly, she was intimidated by my imposing physique."

"That's probably what it was," Sera said. "Why don't you let me do the talking from now on?"

Dak shrugged. He had to admit that Sera did a better

job of blending in here. "Suit yourself. Anyway, it sure seems like a lot of people are heading up to the cave. Are you thinking what I'm thinking?"

"What?"

"That we should follow them, check out what's going on?"

Sera put her hands on her hips and looked away from Dak for a few seconds. He followed her eyes down the alley where two Franciscan monks were walking side by side in stuffy-looking robes. "We can't just leave Riq," Sera said.

"We're not leaving him," Dak told her. "We're just momentarily suspending our search. Besides, isn't this mission bigger than any one person? That's what Riq always says. Just because he's off somewhere pining over Medusa doesn't mean the rest of us are supposed to stop working."

Sera was staring at Dak with a sad expression on her face. Like she felt sorry for him. He'd caught her staring at him this way a number of times since they landed here. He didn't understand. Why would anyone feel sorry for him? Was it because of his parents? Sure, it was rotten luck they'd been lost in the river of time, but they'd be reunited. And in the meantime he was busy living history, fixing it where it needed to be fixed. "Look," Dak said, breaking eye contact, "I promise we'll come right back down. Unless you wanna stick around for a conversation with *those* guys." He motioned toward the monks.

"Fine," Sera said. "We'll go check it out, then we're coming right back down here and finding Riq."

Dak pumped his fist a few times, then waved for Sera to follow him. He didn't know what to expect from a secret Mayan meeting, but it was bound to be worth seeing.

Dak and Sera climbed the boulders in front of the cave and took a few steps inside. The musty smell brought back a slew of memories for Dak. He remembered waking up on the makeshift cot with a man wearing feathers, burning herbs over his chest. He remembered watching Sera's lips move as she spoke to him in words he couldn't quite hear. But mostly he remembered the strange visions he'd had throughout his recovery. There was the one where he was trapped inside a well. Or the one where he was climbing through a cramped tunnel that never seemed to end. But the strangest vision of all was the one where Sera had come to him and revealed that Itchik was her father.

Dak peeked at Sera now as she studied the several dozen Mayas gathered inside the cave. If Sera traced her family tree back far enough, he wondered if it would lead her all the way back to this very village.

"All right, my good people," a young Mayan man suddenly announced. "Bring it in a little tighter, please." They moved deeper inside the cave, some of them holding candles or masks or food offerings.

Sera led Dak behind a large limestone sculpture, where they were hidden. "We can listen for a few minutes," she whispered, "but then we're going back to find Riq."

"Fine," Dak whispered back.

"As you all know," the man continued, "there are rumors that Diego de Landa will physically punish anyone caught paying respect to our spiritual ancestors. We have begun to meet in these caves because the monks believe they are haunted. That provides us some measure of safety. Any newcomers, tonight you will join us in honoring Ah Mun, Chan K'uh, Chaac, K'inich Ajaw, and many others. In our traditional ways. Because this is who we are, yes?"

Dak watched everyone nod and echo, "This is who we are." He'd never seen anything like it.

"Good," the man said. "Now pull out whatever you have brought, and let us begin."

Anyone who had a bag reached into it now and pulled out some type of artifact. Dak saw them produce codices, masks, figurines, elaborate costumes and headdresses, incense sticks, detailed tapestries.

"They might be able to change the way we believe out there," the man said, pointing outside the cave, "but they can never change the way we believe in here." He tapped his thumb against his chest several times and repeated, "Never in here."

Without any further direction, the Mayas all began

chanting together and dancing. A few held masks up to their faces and bowed to the people around them.

Dak turned to Sera and whispered, "You heard what he said is going on, right? Diego de Landa is a Franciscan monk known for traveling to the most remote Mayan villages to try to convert all the indigenous people to Christianity. According to most historical accounts, he was the single most influential figure in the suppression of Mayan—"

"Be quiet, Dak," Sera interrupted. "Just watch and listen. Maybe you'll learn something."

Dak grinned. "Look who's starting to admire the Maya," he whispered.

They both spun around quickly when they heard voices coming from the opening of the cave. Dak saw five large men, dressed much differently than the Mayas, peering in at the processions. They didn't seem to notice Dak and Sera hiding behind the sculpture. One of the men pointed at the Mayas and nodded, and they all moved into the cave together.

Dak pushed down Sera's head and ducked himself so the men wouldn't see them as they passed by.

One of the Spaniards shouted at the Mayas, "Every one of you must come with us. There's no use trying to get away." Each of the five men produced either cross-bows or muskets.

The chanting and dancing immediately stopped.

Many of the Mayas held up their hands and surrendered peacefully, but others sprinted toward the cave exit, pushing past the Spaniards on their way by, knocking two of the men over. The three men who remained standing opened fire on the fleeing Mayas. One young Mayan man fell onto his stomach when an arrow pierced his back. He hopped back up and staggered a few more steps, and then collapsed back onto the ground.

The surrendered Mayas all gasped as the injured man went still.

Sera made a move for the dying man, but Dak grabbed her arm and pulled her back. "They can't know we're here," he whisper-shouted.

Sera turned her glassy eyes toward Dak but said nothing.

"Let's make this easy, folks," one of the Spaniards announced. "We don't want any more casualties."

The Mayas were all led out of the cave in connected shackles, heads bowed. The injustice of it all bubbled inside Dak's chest. All they had been doing was celebrating their history. Dak could relate; history was everything to him, too. What if someone shot at him for studying the second Roman Empire?

He watched one of the Spaniards shove the last Mayas toward the exit of the cave and then they were gone. They had just left the dead Mayan man to rot.

"They killed him!" Sera cried, stepping out from behind the limestone sculpture. "And we did nothing!"

"What could we have done?" Dak said.

Sera knelt down beside the fallen man and closed his eyelids. "And for what?" she said, choking up as she spoke. "What did he die for?"

Dak knelt beside her. "It isn't fair," he said. "Maybe this is why we're here, Sera. To make sure the Maya are no longer treated this way. Or maybe we're here to change the way they're perceived by future generations."

Sera didn't say anything. She just kept staring down at the man, shaking her head.

Dak moved deeper into the cave. He picked up one of the colorful masks and studied the details. Then he knelt down and flipped through several codices lying in the clay dirt. None of them had a painting of a ceiba tree. He moved over to a large wooden box filled with smaller masks and figurines and traditional-looking jewelry. He picked up a paintbrush, then a colorfully painted ceramic, an old locket similar to the one Kisa had tried to give Riq. Then he found several small ceramic instruments that resembled modern drums and flutes.

"Leave me alone!" Sera suddenly shouted.

Dak spun around to find a large Spanish man restraining Sera's hands behind her back. The man looked up at Dak and said, "Let's go, boy. Don't make it any harder than it has to be."

Sera tried to wrestle away from the man, but he whacked her in the back of the head with an elbow and tightened her restraints.

"Don't touch her!" Dak shouted.

"Then get over here!" the man shouted back.

Dak reached back into the box and dug around for the locket. He pulled it out and hid it in his breechcloth as he stood up.

The Spaniard was already shoving Sera toward Dak and readying a second restraint.

1 4

Wisdom in a Prison Cell

"IN YOU go!" a Spanish guard shouted, shoving Sera and Dak into a large cell that already held dozens of Mayas—many of whom Sera had just seen inside the cave.

"You killed my brother!" a Mayan girl shrieked, running toward the open door.

"Not me personally," the man said, grinning. "But maybe one of my colleagues."

Another guard held the girl back with a long club. "Brother de Landa warned you about practicing your witchcraft. But do any of you listen? No." He slammed closed the door and locked it, shouting through the sliding peephole, "There's a price to pay for choosing the devil's path!"

The guards left, and the young Mayan leader from the cave helped the sobbing girl up and led her to the one bench in the room. He cleared away the people sitting there and had the girl lie down. Then he knelt and took her hands into his and spoke to her in a hushed tone Sera couldn't quite make out.

Sera took in her surroundings. The cell was half underground. There were barred windows on three of the walls, a little above eye level, and through them Sera could only see a small portion of the sky, which was turning dark.

An older Mayan man approached Dak and Sera, and stood there with his arms crossed. "What is the most important thing in the world?" he asked.

"What?" Dak said. He turned to Sera and mouthed, "The riddle!"

"I know," Sera mouthed back.

"Just as I suspected," the Mayan man said. "You don't have an answer."

"No, we do!" Dak shouted. "The most important thing in the world is . . . corn?"

The man scoffed and moved away from Dak and Sera.

"Asymmetrical tortillas?" Dak called out after him.

The man didn't even turn around.

Sera led Dak to an empty corner of the cell.

"That question was right out of the riddle," Dak said. "We just have to figure out the answer and we'll be a step closer to solving it."

Sera leaned her back against the dirty prison wall and let herself slide down to a sitting position, her face falling into her hands. She'd never felt so defeated in her life. Or depressed. She was only eleven years old. Wasn't eleven too young to process the things she'd experienced over the past twenty-four hours? The realization that she'd found her parents facedown in her flooded barn. Watching a man get taken down by an arrow when he didn't even do anything. Being thrown into a prison. She couldn't stand the way the Mayas were treated by the monks. How could a foreign people come waltzing into someone else's village and start telling them what to believe? To make things worse, the Mayas didn't trust her and Dak just because they didn't know some secret code word.

Dak sat down next to her. "We'll be okay, Sera."

She looked up at him. "Will we, Dak? Because I'm not so sure anymore."

He pointed at her satchel holding the Infinity Ring. "You still have the Ring, and I have the SQuare. We can use this time to regroup and figure out the riddle."

Sera shook her head. "What's the point, Dak? Are we really making a difference?"

"Of course we are," Dak said. "What's going on? You usually have such a good attitude."

Sera paused, fighting the lump in her throat. "I've been doing a lot of thinking, Dak. We're not actually *fixing* history at all. We're not making anything better for anyone." She motioned toward the Mayas. "They just want to live their lives and learn about the world and follow their traditions. And they can't even sneak off to a cave to honor what they believe in? One of them has to pay with his life?"

"We already talked about this," Dak said. He looked away from Sera for a few seconds, like he was thinking. Sera saw over his shoulder that the Mayan leader was now pacing the cell. "The point of fixing the Breaks," Dak said, "isn't to make history more morally correct."

"Why not?" Sera said. "Why aren't we trying to make the world a better place?"

Dak shrugged. "I don't know, Sera. Sometimes we are, I think. But we're just two kids. Two and a half, if you count Lover Boy. The point is, we're sent to each place to fix a Break, not humanity."

"So you don't ever question it?"

"No, I do," Dak said. "But at the end of the day I trust the Hystorians. They've been working to avert the Cataclysm and defeat the SQ longer than we've been alive."

Sera stared at Dak. She wanted to come right out and tell him—how she'd been given a glimpse of the unspeakable Cataclysm. But she couldn't. She had to keep this cancerous knowledge to herself.

Sera grabbed at her own hair and pulled, saying, "I don't know if I can go on, Dak. I really don't."

"But you have to," the Mayan leader said. "And you will."

Sera looked up, saw the young man now hovering

over her and Dak, his fists clenched. "There will always be injustice," he continued. "In all things. And many times we will not be able to alter these things. But what we can *always* do is lift our heads and continue on. That part is in our control."

Sera felt embarrassed that the man had overheard her whining. She must've sounded like a spoiled brat.

"They can lock us behind these walls," the man said, shaking the bars in the window to the left of Sera and Dak. "All of us. The entire village. But in our minds we will always remain free. Remember that." He reached a hand out and helped Sera to her feet, saying, "I am Bacab."

"Sera," she answered, trying to seem as respectful as possible. Because she already admired the man. She'd seen how all the people in the cave, many of them much older, were hanging on his every word.

Dak elbowed Sera in the arm and cleared his throat.

"Oh," she said, "and this is my friend Dak."

"Hi," Dak said.

"A pleasure to meet you both," Bacab said. "You're not from around here, obviously. But where you come from does not concern me. It is where you are now that matters. And that is with us."

Sera glanced over at the rest of the Mayas. A few of them didn't seem as eager to accept her and Dak — probably because they didn't know the answer to the question from the riddle.

"So, how do we get out of here?" Dak asked.

"We have our ways," Bacab said. "This is my fourth time inside this very cell. What they fail to understand is that I have a key in my room. Late this evening, my younger brother will realize I'm not home. The first place he will check is the prison cell. And he knows to bring the key."

"Wait . . . you have a key?" Dak said.

Bacab grinned. "When I'm not organizing our gatherings, I work as a locksmith."

Seeing the young man's grin made Sera feel better. She, too, wanted to be the kind of person who could grin in the face of adversity.

"We can't remain here long," a second Mayan man said. "If the great storm comes as predicted, it will flood the cell. They will leave us to drown."

"No one here is going to drown," Bacab said. He turned back to Dak and Sera, and said, "This is my younger cousin, K'inich. He is an excellent locksmith's assistant, and he has traveled extensively, but he worries too much."

"Wait, there's supposed to be another great storm?" Dak said. He banged on the stone wall with the heel of his hand. "Sure hope these bad boys are built stronger than they used to be."

Bacab lifted Sera's chin so that their eyes met. "Young sister," he said, "you have questions swimming in your eyes."

"I don't know," she said, embarrassed that she looked so uncertain. "Why are they even doing this? You weren't hurting anyone tonight."

"The monks are frustrated. Their plan is to take over every village, from sea to sea, but in order to do this peacefully and efficiently, they must first convert my people to their religion. Then we will believe the land is theirs by divine right, you see?"

"So that's why you gathered in the cave," Sera said.

"That and the acoustics make my voice sound nice," Bacab said with another grin.

"They've been threatening us," K'inich said. "Diego de Landa, one of the leaders of the Franciscan monks, says if we don't obey he will get rid of everything we hold sacred."

"Oh, wow," Dak said. "I've totally read about this. That de Landa dude gets so mad he orders an *auto-da-fe*, where he—"

Sera stepped on Dak's foot to cut him off.

"Ow!" Dak shrieked.

"You're speculating, of course," Sera said, shooting Dak a dirty look.

"Oh. Right." Dak turned to Bacab. "What I meant to say is, aren't you guys afraid something bad might happen to your codices and stuff?"

Sera noticed that K'inich was staring at Dak. "How could you know something that has yet to happen?" he asked.

"No, I don't," Dak said. "I was just . . . sometimes I get my verb tenses confused."

"My hope is that a highly spiritual man like de Landa," Bacab said, "would never stoop so low as confiscating our history."

"Well, I wouldn't hope too hard," Dak said quietly, so only Sera could hear.

K'inich was whispering something into Bacab's ear now. Sera pulled Dak aside and said, "Maybe this is the Break we're supposed to fix." After talking with Bacab she felt suddenly reenergized, like she was ready to fight again. Maybe this was the mark of a great leader.

"That's it," Dak nearly shouted. "We have to stop de Landa's *auto-da-fe*."

Sera put a finger to her lips for Dak to lower his voice. "So, at some point are you planning to explain what the heck an *auto-da-fe* is?" she said. "Or do you just enjoy hearing yourself say it?"

"*Auto-da-fe. Auto-da-fe. Auto-da-fe.*" Dak smiled. "Just kidding, dude. An *auto-da-fe* is —"

Before Dak could finish, a few of the Mayas got up suddenly and started converging around the far window. Bacab and K'inich hurried over to join them.

Sera and Dak stood on their tiptoes near the back of the crowd to try to see what was going on. All Sera could see was the bottom portion of a monk's robe on the other side of the window. Someone was there.

And that someone was now kneeling down to look inside the cell.

Sera's eyes widened.

It was Riq.

Dressed like a Franciscan monk.

"What do you want?" one of the Mayas barked at him.

"To speak with Dak and Sera," Riq said. "I'm not an actual monk, I promise."

"Riq!" Sera shouted over the crowd.

"Why should we believe you?" another Mayan man said.

Sera started pushing through the pack. If she could just get to him, she could explain. Dak suddenly weaseled right past her, though, and lunged for the window, holding out a piece of jewelry. Riq reached his hand through the narrow bars and took it.

"It looks like the one you lost!" Dak shouted. "I thought maybe you'd want it!"

"Thanks," Riq said, slipping it into the bag hanging off of the rope belt of his robe.

"Why are you here?" a woman shouted at Riq. "Haven't you people done enough for one night?"

Several other Mayas began peppering Riq with questions, too, until Bacab shouted, "Silence!"

The entire cell went quiet.

"Thank you," Bacab said. "Let me ask the boy our question before we proceed any further." The Mayas nodded and made a path for Bacab to get to the window. As he wrapped his hands around the bars, he looked up at Riq and said, "What is the most important thing in the world, young man?"

Sera watched Riq look to the ground, confused. She was about to move toward the window so she could explain that they weren't from around here, when Riq suddenly raised his eyes to Bacab and said, "Friendship."

All at once the Mayas looked at one another, nodding, and began reaching their arms through the bars to shake hands with Riq.

Sera turned to Dak, who was already staring at her with a puzzled look on his face. He motioned toward Riq and said, "What the . . . ?"

Sera shrugged and told him, "You took the words right out of my mouth."

A Necessary Detour

As Riq hurried away from the subterranean prison cell, he kept repeating in his head the name of the boy he'd just been asked to locate, the boy that Bacab claimed would have a key to the cell: *Okib. Okib. Okib.*

He couldn't allow himself to forget.

But at the same time he was also thinking about the ancient locket Dak had handed him through the prison bars. It was the only reason he'd been able to answer Bacab's strange question. In a conversation with Kisa, he remembered telling her that the most important thing in the world was having friends. So he threw it out there to Bacab. But he was completely shocked that he'd gotten it right.

Riq pulled the locket out now as he moved through the village looking for the boy. It was rusted shut, the metal on both sides dull and badly dented. There was no way it was the locket Kisa had tried to give him before he warped away with Dak and Sera. Even if it was, would he actually want it? The girl had done nothing but confuse him. One minute she seemed so excited for him to stay. The next minute she was ordering him out of her village.

Riq was tempted to boot the locket right into the bushes.

He didn't, though.

He slipped it back into his belt's bag and continued repeating the boy's name in his head: *Okib. Okib. Okib.*

Riq had been walking around for a half hour before he spotted a small group of Mayan boys playing on a ball court. He called down to them, "By any chance, is one of you guys named Okib?"

The boys all looked at one another, shaking their heads.

"You sure?" Riq said. "I'm not a real monk, I promise. And I have an important message from Bacab." He wished he could ditch the Franciscan robe he was wearing. It was making the kids nervous.

"He might be getting stuff out of the cave," one of the boys offered.

"Did something bad happen?" another boy asked.

"I don't think so," Riq said, not wanting to alarm them. "Bacab just asked that I find Okib."

"You should try the cave," the first boy said.

Riq thanked them and started in the direction of

the path that would lead him to the cave. He looked down at his robe, feeling entirely out of place. When he left Dak and Sera earlier, he had ducked into the church to be alone and saw the robe hanging over a chair. He'd changed into it without much thought . . . other than he no longer wanted to be wearing the clothes he'd worn when he knew Kisa. A new outfit, he had told himself, might help give him a fresh perspective.

It didn't, of course. He left the church feeling just as confused as ever.

Kisa must have realized something truly awful about him to change her mind so quickly. Riq pulled the locket out again. He just needed to get rid of it. All it did was remind him of what happened.

Instead of hurling it into the bushes, though, he fired it at the ground, as hard as he could. Then he sat down on a boulder and looked up into the sky. The moon and stars were out, and he thought how it was the same moon and stars that had hovered over Izamal almost one thousand years ago. The sky didn't need a time machine to witness all that went on in the world, which included the time he'd spent with Kisa.

The air was warm and humid. Far off to the east he saw storm clouds. He watched them for a few seconds, trying to determine how quickly they were approaching, then he shifted his attention back to the locket on the ground.

He was surprised to see that it had broken into two pieces.

He walked over and picked them up, and stared at the inside of the back half where a single glyph had been written: *observatory*. The handwriting reminded him of the message Kisa had carved into the boulder when she'd left him the snake bracelet.

Riq got chills as he looked up at the tall observatory.

Could it really be Kisa trying to send him a message?

The path that led up to the cave was just past the observatory. If Riq hurried, he could take a quick look inside before heading up the hill.

He shoved the locket pieces back into his bag and took off running.

The two monks near the front entrance didn't pay Riq any mind, most likely because of the robe he was wearing. He was able to duck right inside the huge observatory and check things out. It was quite old though still functioning. Parts of the walls were peeling and cracked. The center of the ground floor was flat, and the roof was open at the very top so that Riq could see the sky. All around the main part of the observatory were doors, maybe a dozen of them.

Riq knew what he was doing was insane — trying to figure out the meaning of a single-glyph clue written almost one thousand years ago. Or maybe it wasn't a clue at all. Maybe it had been written by someone other than Kisa. Or what if Kisa had left the clue for someone else? This version of the observatory didn't even exist yet when she'd tried to hand him the locket.

Another question started circling through his head: Why would a girl give a clue to someone she didn't even want around?

Riq moved around the interior of the observatory anyway, opening every door, peering inside. They were mostly small rooms with new desks and chairs. Three of the doors were locked. One led to a staircase. Riq took the skinny stairs all the way up to the ceiling and looked back down at the ground floor, trying to figure out what might be significant about an observatory. But it was all so ordinary.

There was a thin walkway up near the dome. He stepped out onto it, moved carefully around every inch looking for some other kind of clue. But it was just a walkway. Nothing more. He eventually climbed back down the stairs, passing the ground floor and ducking into the basement. He opened the door and felt his way down the dark hallway, sliding his hands against the wall. He tried a door along the way that was locked. Then he saw that there was an open room at the far end of the hall . . . with what looked like candlelight flickering within.

Riq walked faster through the darkness and peeked

inside. There were three women sitting on simple wooden chairs, sorting through wooden boxes. One looked up at Riq, her eyes growing wide with surprise. "Who are you?" she demanded, dropping what looked like another locket inside the box. "And what are you doing in here?"

All three women picked up their sewing and stood up, kicking the boxes behind their feet.

"We've been cleared by Brother de Landa to do our embroideries in here," the shortest of them said.

"They're for the church," the first woman added.

"Don't worry," Riq told the women, "I'm not a real monk. I was just looking for a girl." It was clear they weren't doing anything for the church.

"A girl?" the short woman asked. "No one is allowed to be down here but the three of us with our embroidery."

"A woman, I mean," Riq corrected himself. "She lived a long, long time ago. Her name was Kisa."

The women all looked at one another, shaking their heads.

"Her uncle was King Itchik," Riq added. "I believe he was responsible for building this observatory."

"I've never heard of anyone named Kisa," the short woman said. "Or a King Itchik for that matter. Have you?" she asked her friends.

"Never," they both said.

The taller woman glanced at the box behind her. Then she turned back to Riq and lowered her eyes. He saw that she had a large birthmark on the right side of her face.

Riq nodded. "Thanks for your help—"

"Where are you from?" the woman with the birthmark said, cutting him off.

"Me?" Riq said. He didn't quite know how to answer. "Well, I'm from . . . a faraway village."

The woman continued staring at him. "And what is the name of this village?"

Riq leaned against the wall behind him and said, "Oh, it's very small. Most people have never heard of it."

The other two women were looking at the woman with the birthmark.

"Anyway," Riq said, pushing off the wall, "I'm sorry to have disturbed you."

The women remained standing in front of their boxes until Riq left the room.

He hurried back up the stairs and out of the observatory, trying to forget about the cryptic message inside the locket and the women and the fact that there may be additional lockets inside those wooden boxes they were hiding. Right now he needed to concentrate on finding the boy Bacab had asked him to find.

Riq started up the dark path, toward the cave, when he collided suddenly with someone hurrying back down the path.

They both tumbled into the bushes.

Riq, slightly dazed, raised his head to find a boy lying

in the bushes beside him. "Okib?" he asked hesitantly.

The boy sat up and looked at him.

Riq remembered his robe and said, "Don't worry, I'm not a real monk. But is it really you, Okib?"

The boy shrugged and looked around.

Riq scrambled to his feet and leaned down over the boy. "A man named Bacab asked me to find you. He's in the village holding cell with two of my friends, and he claims you'll know what to do."

The boy stood up. He looked about Dak's age. "I knew it!" he cried.

"Knew what?" Riq asked.

"There was nothing left in the cave." The boy wiped a hand down his face. "They took it all. Everything."

"Someone stole from you?" Riq asked.

"The monks did," the boy said. "Why won't they just leave us alone? We're not hurting anyone."

Riq felt the injustice in his chest. "Come," he told the boy. "I'll take you to Bacab."

"No," Okib said. "My brother says I must always wait until deep into the night, when everyone has fallen asleep. Then I will bring him the key."

Riq looked out over Izamal. For the first time since they arrived in this new time period, he wondered about the Break they needed to fix. He'd been moping around long enough. It was time to get back to his life's work: being a Hystorian. "Follow me," he told Okib, with a new sense of determination. "We can wait inside the observatory. You tell me when the time is right to free your people, and I will come along to assist you."

Okib looked up at him, nodding.

They started back down the path together, Riq gripping the locket pieces in his satchel and promising himself he would remain absolutely focused for the remainder of the mission.

The Other Hystorians

DAK WAS half-asleep and completely aware that he was dreaming, but the dream was a good one so he kept his eyes closed and followed along with the story. He was at Sera's birthday party, just outside her barn, and her uncle had just blindfolded him and handed him a stick. He spun Dak around several times and then let go, saying, "Let her rip!" Dak staggered a little, dizzy, then started hacking at the swinging piñata, which he knew was somewhere in front of him.

He missed twice, then connected on his third try.

On his fourth swing, he reared back and whacked the piñata with all his strength, feeling the side cave in. He could hear the candy start pouring out.

When Dak ripped off the blindfold, he saw that it wasn't candy at all. It was blocks of high-end cheese. All different kinds and sizes. They looked beautiful streaming out onto the thick summer grass. The other kids were already converging with their empty pillowcases, scooping the cheese blocks up with two hands and shoving them inside, and Dak shouted, "Hey, wait for me! I have to get my pillowcase!" But he couldn't find his pillowcase, not anywhere, and all the while more and more kids raced past him, pouncing on what was left from the piñata *he* broke open.

"Wake up," he heard Sera whispering in his ear.

"But they're taking all my cheese," he told her.

"Dak, wake up!" she whispered louder this time.

He opened his eyes, and he saw all the imprisoned Mayas quietly filing out the open door of the prison cell. Sera pulled him to his feet and they joined the line, and soon they were sneaking past two sleeping monks, ducking out of the building, and hurrying into the night.

Dak followed Sera over to where Riq was standing. Riq pointed toward the towering observatory, and without saying a word, the three of them split off from the others and hurried through the village in that direction.

As they ran, Dak kept looking all around, worried someone might hop out of the bushes and snatch them up. He saw several monks milling around in the square, though it was too dark to see what they were doing. He saw a giant wooden cross leaning up against one of the huts. He saw storm clouds gathering in the distant sky.

Riq opened the observatory doors, ushered Dak and Sera inside, then led them to the far corner of the large room where Dak glanced up at the open roof. The three of them stood there for several quiet seconds, hands on knees, trying to catch their breath and looking all around them.

Sera was the first to straighten back up. She took in a deep breath and said to Riq, "How'd you know the answer was *friendship*?"

Riq took his hands off his knees, too. "A conversation I had with Kisa," he said, linking his fingers on top of his head and taking a few more deep breaths.

Dak pulled the SQuare out of his breechcloth and said, "Dude, that was almost a thousand years ago. How could it possibly apply to today?"

Riq shook his head. "Trust me, I was just as surprised as you guys."

Dak powered on the SQuare and brought up the latest riddle — which Riq had yet to see. "Before we look at this I just want to say something, okay? It seems like something really messed up is happening here. Something other than the Break." Dak looked at Sera. "Once we fix what we're supposed to fix, if you guys want to help these people in some other way, I'm totally open to that."

Sera gave him a small smile and said, "Thanks, Dak. Let's concentrate on the Break for now. We can discuss everything else later on."

Dak realized it was the first time he'd seen Sera smile in a long time. "I just know it's important to you," he said.

"It is."

Riq cleared his throat. "I wanted to say something, too. It was wrong of me to just wander off like that. I apologize. I also want to assure you I'm as committed to our mission as I've ever been."

"We know you are," Sera said.

Dak patted Riq on the shoulder. "It's cool, dude. Just remember, love is a tricky game—"

"Moving right along," Sera said, pointing at the SQuare in Dak's hand.

"Oh. Right." Dak turned the screen around so Riq and Sera could see. "We were thinking you might be able to help us with this second riddle, Riq." Dak silently reread the words upside down:

To save the reproduction of the treasure's truth, do the following
Seek the help of those who follow "the most important thing in the world"
Then dig deep, deeper, deepest, unlocking a long-locked door
It will take a polyglot to understand the wisdom of the glyphs
and the forgery of the curse

"So, we're supposed to find people who follow friend-ship," Riq said.

"Apparently, we already did," Dak said. "Everyone in the holding cell knew the answer to that question. Well, everyone but Sera."

"Ha-ha," Sera said, rolling her eyes. "All of the Mayas

in the cell had been in the cave earlier, too. Which means they're proud of their Mayan roots, right?"

"Exactly." Dak turned to Riq and said, "We learned from Bacab that the monks have caused a split among the Mayan people. Some are embracing the Spanish influence. Others want to remain loyal to ancient Mayan ways."

"So, this Break," Sera said, pointing at Dak, "has to center around something they have stashed in that cave. Most likely —"

"Pacal's codex," Dak said.

"It's not in the cave anymore," Riq said. "According to Bacab's little brother, everything's been cleared out. He told me the monks confiscated it all."

Dak smacked his own forehead with the heel of his hand. "Dude, I just realized something. Did you guys see the monks in the square on the way over here?"

Riq and Sera both nodded.

Dak turned to Riq. "Back in the cell, Bacab explained that every hut with a secret friendship sculpture out front was storing ancient Mayan artifacts. The problem is, over the past several weeks they've been transferring everything up to the cave. They thought that would be safer."

Sera's eyes grew big. "They're piling everything into the square!" she shouted. "They're planning to burn it."

"Bingo," Dak said. "And that bonfire, my friend, is what's otherwise known as an *auto-da-fe*."

They all just stared at one another, mouths hanging

open in shock, until Dak said, "We have to stop it. Pacal's codex has to be preserved. That's gotta be the Break, right? Which means the one that has survived history is a fake!"

Sera took the SQuare out of Dak's hands and held it out to Riq. "Do you understand anything else in the riddle?"

"A *polyglot* is someone who can speak or write multiple languages," he said, looking up at Sera.

"Like you, dude," Dak said.

Riq nodded.

"So, we need Riq's language ability," Sera said, "in order to understand the wisdom of the glyphs and the forgery of the curse." She patted Riq on the back. "We're sure glad you came back."

Dak sensed Riq might be feeling a little too good about himself. He opened his mouth to say something sarcastic, but just then he heard someone entering through the front door of the observatory. Dak snatched the SQuare from Sera and shoved it back into his breechcloth.

"Quick," Riq said. "Follow me." He pulled a candle out of its holder on the wall and started toward one of the doors.

Dak and Sera followed Riq through the door and down a narrow staircase. Then the three of them crept slowly through a dark hall, Riq leading the way with his candle. Dak wasn't sure the basement was the best idea until he spotted an open door at the opposite end.

Riq stopped right in front of it, waiting for Dak and Sera to catch up. Then the three of them looked inside. There was a tall Mayan woman sitting in a chair, holding a wooden box in her lap and grinning. Dak saw she had a birthmark on her cheek.

"I've been waiting for you three," she said.

Dak let Riq and Sera take the two empty chairs and he stood behind them, studying the Mayan woman and the wooden box in her lap. There were a number of ancient Mayan artifacts inside — including several lockets that resembled the one he'd given to Riq. The woman got up to close the door, and then sat back down and said, "I'm just going to come out and ask: Are you from the future?"

Dak, Sera, and Riq all looked at one another, then Dak turned back to the woman and said, "We are, ma'am."

The woman covered her mouth, and her eyes turned glassy. "I knew it," she said, pointing at Riq. "As soon as you showed up earlier this evening, in that ill-fitting robe, I had this strange feeling in my stomach." She shook her head and said, "Wow. I did not expect to be having *this* conversation tonight."

"My turn to ask a question," Dak said. "Are you a Hystorian?"

"I am."

"What about those two other ladies?" Riq asked. "The ones you were sitting with earlier."

"No, it's just me now." She covered her mouth again, briefly, then took a deep breath and said, "Forgive me. I just . . . I never thought I'd actually live to see the day."

"Finally," Dak said, turning to Sera and Riq. "I was beginning to think there weren't any Hystorians in all of Mesoamerica."

"Oh, no," the woman said. "We're here. Just extremely spread out. In fact, this region is actually the birthplace of the Hystorian presence in the Americas."

"The first Hystorian in the Americas was Mayan?" Sera said. "Who? When?"

"An amazing woman known as Akna," she answered. "A long, long time ago. By the way, I'm María."

"María?" Dak said. "That doesn't sound very Mayan to me."

"It's not. My parents passed away when I was an infant, and I was raised by Spanish nuns. They're the ones who named me. When I got older I began researching my Mayan roots, which is how I stumbled into the underground Hystorian movement. I joined immediately, hoping I could help make tomorrow's world a better and safer place."

Dak, Sera, and Riq introduced themselves to María, and then Riq pulled two locket pieces out of the bag on his belt and held them out. "I came in here earlier because of this."

"Dude, you broke my gift," Dak said. "That hurts."

"See what's written inside there?" Riq said, turning the locket toward Dak.

"How about a little help?" Dak said. "You know I can't read glyphs."

Riq turned the locket halves toward María, who said a single word: "Observatory."

"We were in this same village a long time ago," Riq told her, "and I knew a girl named Kisa. She tried to give me a locket like this one when we were leaving, but I dropped it. That's why I was asking about her earlier tonight. So, you're sure you've never heard of her?"

María shook her head and told him, "But I need to show you something fascinating." She dug into the wooden box, pulling out several similar-looking ancient lockets. "Each of you take one and open it up," she said.

Dak opened his and looked at the glyph inside. It was exactly like the one Riq had just shown him.

Riq and Sera held out their open lockets, too.

"They all say 'observatory,'" Riq said.

"We are constantly finding more and more lockets," María said. "And they all have the same word inside. We still don't understand why."

Sera set her locket down. "Kisa was really trying to tell you something, Riq."

He shrugged but didn't say anything. Dak could tell the guy was feeling all sensitive again. He made a mental note to lead Riq through a quick seminar on love, as soon as they could carve out the free time.

"We always assumed the author of these messages was Akna," María said. "That is why previous Hystorians established the observatory as their base. According to legend, Akna was so committed to our cause she worked all the way up until the day she passed away from old age."

"Whoever wrote it," Dak said. "Why were they being so vague?"

"She probably worried the information would get into the wrong hands," Sera said. "Where there are Hystorians, there are usually Time Wardens, too."

"Of course," María said. Then she stood up. "Come with me. I'd like to show the three of you something else."

Dak, Sera, and Riq followed María halfway down the hall, until she stopped, knelt down, and shone her candlelight on a lower portion of the wall. She felt with her fingers along the wall until she came to a small keyhole. "I've never mentioned this to anyone," she said, looking up. "There's a locked door here. It's been this way at least as far back as I go. But we believe there's a secret room behind this wall. According to legend, it was the meeting place of the first-ever Hystorians in this part of the world, led, of course, by our remarkable founder, Akna."

Dak saw two tiny snakes were carved into the stone near the keyhole. "Check it out," he said.

Sera turned to Riq, who had tensed at the sight. "Could two people be that into snakes?" she asked.

"We have to get inside," Riq said.

Sera nodded. "The riddle says we're supposed to unlock a long-locked door," she said. "This has to be it."

Dak pressed on the small stone door, then tried to rattle it. "Deep, deeper, deepest," he said. He was getting excited, thinking about all the Hystorian history that might be on the other side of the stone wall. "Talk to us, María. How do we open this bad boy?"

"There is no key," María said. "Many generations of Hystorians have stood in this very place, wishing they could see what's inside. But locked out we have remained."

"Bacab!" Dak shouted, springing to his feet. "We have to track that dude down ASAP! He's a locksmith!"

The Way Events Unfolded

IT DIDN'T take long for Sera to see what the Mayan people were up against.

As she, Dak, and Riq hurried away from the observatory, they passed the village square, where several Franciscan monks were tossing ancient Mayan artifacts onto a massive pile. It was dawn now so Sera could see it all clearly. A few monks were tucking kindling into the pile. Two dozen or so armed Spanish men stood in a circle around the monks, almost daring village locals to interfere. Sera noticed that all the guards from the prison were part of the circle. So were the men who'd forced the Mayas out of the cave.

One monk seemed to be overseeing the entire operation.

Sera studied him as they moved past the scene. She knew he must be the infamous Diego de Landa.

Bacab wasn't at his hut.

They found him at a nearby ball court, huddled with several other Mayan men, including his younger cousin, K'inich.

"Bacab," Sera said, half out of breath, "have you seen what the monks are doing in the square?"

"I know what they're doing, little sister." He turned around, showing the crossbow in his hands. "It is why we are preparing for battle."

"But they're sitting there waiting for you!" Sera shouted.

"And they're heavily armed," Riq added.

"If they try to burn our history, we will stand up against them," Bacab said. He grinned at Sera. "I'm not afraid to risk my life for what's right." Then he turned back to his men and began barking instructions.

She spun around to face Dak and Riq. "I have to help them," she said.

"Sera, we need you," Riq said.

"The best way to help them," Dak said, "is to fix this Break. We can change the way the world perceives the Mayan people forever."

Sera was so confused. She felt a strange, unexplainable loyalty toward these people — like they were family. And if they were willing to risk their lives, she felt like she should, too. But the rational side of Sera knew Dak was right. If they fixed the Break, made sure the right codex survived the burning, the Maya would no longer be famous for declaring the SQ saviors of the world. Maybe instead they'd be celebrated for their actual wisdom and . . . scientific achievements. Sera never thought she'd consider the Maya scientific, but that's exactly what they were.

She turned back to Bacab. "We need your help getting into a room in the observatory."

"Can it wait until after our battle in the square?" K'inich said, frowning at her. "You may have noticed, Bacab is a little preoccupied at the moment."

"I'm sorry, but it can't wait," Sera said flatly. "Bacab, do you have keys to the doors in the observatory basement?"

"If it is a lock in this village," Bacab said, "I have the key."

"And what is in the basement?" K'inich asked.

"There's a room we think might be very important to us," Dak said.

Bacab stood there, looking out over the horizon. "It would be much easier if this could wait."

"Or you could just give us the keys," Dak suggested. "We'd bring them back as soon as we were done."

"Only a locksmith handles a locksmith's keys," Bacab said.

"I will take them," K'inich said, tossing down the coil of rope he'd been holding. He picked up his crossbow and said, "Bacab, you stay here and continue your preparations. I will hurry back."

"You'll really take us?" Dak asked.

"Obviously you are desperate," K'inich said. "So, we will go."

"You know where the keys are," Bacab said. "Come back as soon as you can. We will need every man this morning."

K'inich took off in a jog toward Bacab's hut.

Sera, Dak, and Riq were right on his heels.

K'inich was a very calm and composed man. That was what stood out most to Sera as they walked past the village square on their way back to the observatory. Dak and Riq were a few steps behind, talking. So Sera was free to watch K'inich as he studied the Spanish men guarding the pile of Mayan artifacts. He showed no emotion.

"Doesn't it bother you?" Sera asked him.

"It bothers me very much," K'inich said. "Because it is unjust and ignorant. They do not wish to tolerate what they do not understand."

Sera shook her head. "If I had that crossbow you're wearing, I'd be tempted to fire off a few arrows right about now."

K'inich only smiled at her.

Once the square was well behind them, he said, "I would like to tell you the story of two boys."

It seemed like an odd time to tell a story, but Sera

thought K'inich was intriguing, so she told him, "I'd love to hear a story."

"Wait," Dak said. "What story? We want to hear the story, too."

"Many years ago," K'inich began, "two young boys went out on a raft with one of the most respected elders of their village. This would be both boys' first fishing trip. One of them was the son of the king. The other was a neighborhood boy who the king's son was fond of. They went out into the deeps where the fish were known to bite. The neighborhood boy took to fishing right away. He caught three fish within the first hour. The king's son didn't fare quite as well. He had trouble casting his line. The elder assured him it was simply bad luck. A little while later, the weather began to change."

K'inich paused as he swung open the observatory door and held out his hand for Sera, Dak, and Riq to enter.

"What happened next?" Dak asked as soon as they were all inside.

Sera had no idea how the story applied to anything she'd said, but she was curious, too.

"The elder told the boys they must head for shore right away," K'inich continued. "But the king's son had other ideas. He demanded that they remain in the ocean until he caught a fish, too. He threatened to tell his father if the elder failed to respect his wishes. 'You would lose your standing in the village,' he said. The elder pointed to the swirling sky and told the king's son they were in danger, and he began paddling toward the shore."

They were at the stairs now and K'inich descended them slowly. "On their way in," he said, "the sea grew very rough. A powerful wave rose up and slammed into the wooden raft. The neighborhood boy's fish all washed back into the ocean. Then a second wave appeared, this one bigger and stronger. It picked up the small raft and slammed it back down against the sea. The raft collapsed underneath them, leaving the two boys and the elder alone in the rough water, with nothing to keep them afloat. It was a desperate situation for the elder. Neither boy could swim, and he knew he would only have the strength to save one boy. He turned to them, both thrashing around, fighting to keep their heads above water.

"It was an impossible dilemma. He cared for both boys. But when another large swell rose up in the sea behind them, the elder chose. He grabbed the shirt of the neighborhood boy and held tight as the waves crashed over the top of them, forcing them both underwater. He fought against the current and made it to the surface, holding the boy's face out of the water. Then he swam with his one free hand toward the shore. And eventually they made it."

Sera stopped at the bottom of the stairs. "What happened to the king's son? Did he die?"

"You can't leave us hanging," Dak said.

Sera noticed that Riq seemed far less interested. She tapped the back of his elbow and mouthed, "You okay?"

He nodded.

"The king's son washed ashore several minutes later," K'inich said. "He had drowned. The elder told the truth that night when the king came to see him. He said he understood in the sea that he would only be able to save one boy, and he had chosen the neighborhood boy. The king ordered the elder to be put to death the following morning. Just before the elder was to be sacrificed, the neighborhood boy snuck over to the holding cell, sobbing, and begged the elder to tell him why he hadn't chosen the king's son. And do you know what the elder said?"

"What?" Dak said. "Tell us."

K'inich glanced at Sera and smiled. "He told the boy that he knew the choice he made in the sea would be negative in the short term. He would pay with his life. But in the long term he believed it would prove to be the most beneficial. 'How is that possible?' the boy cried. 'Because tomorrow,' the elder explained, 'you are going to go see a group of people who are very important to me. And you're going to listen to what they have to say. And if my instincts are correct, you will carry their important message into future generations.'"

María came hurrying out of the room at the end

of the hall holding a candle. "You found the key?" she asked.

K'inich held up the massive key ring for her to see, then he began sifting through them, looking for the right one.

Sera watched nervously as the first two keys he tried failed to work.

"So, I must've missed something," Dak said to Sera. "Why was he telling that story?"

"He's right here," Sera said. "Why don't you ask him?"

"How about it, K'inichy?" Dak said.

K'inich was too preoccupied to answer. The third and fourth keys failed as well. But the fifth slid right into the lock and turned easily. K'inich shoved open the heavy stone door, saying, "After you, my friends."

Sera was the first one inside. She expected to see all kinds of Mayan artifacts, but the room was completely empty. She walked to the far wall, studying the floor along the way. It looked like there were fresh drag marks.

"I don't understand," María said. "According to all the records, this is the room."

"Looks like you got some bad intel," Dak said.

Riq tapped Sera on the arm and motioned back at K'inich, who was still hovering by the door. "Are we sure we trust—"

"I'll tell you the point of the story," K'inich interrupted, gripping the top of the door frame.

Everyone turned to look at him.

"Sometimes we must do things that are detrimental in the short term because we know they will prove advantageous in the long term. There is nothing left in this room because I cleared it all out. The artifacts you thought you'd find are at the bottom of the pile in the village square."

María fell to her knees. "What are you saying, K'inich?" she cried.

The realization hit Sera like a ton of bricks. "He's a Time Warden," she said.

Dak started marching toward K'inich with his fists clenched, but K'inich only smiled as he pulled an arrow from the pouch on his shoulder. He loaded it into his crossbow and raised it at Dak, who stopped in his tracks. "I am a proud Maya," K'inich said. "And in the short term, it will be painful to see the legacy of my people turned into ash. See, Diego de Landa will only allow one codex to survive for historical purposes. It shall be the only legacy of the Mayan people. He selected a codex from ancient Izamal, written by a legendary scribe named Pacal. But we have composed our own codex, which reveals the SQ as the rightful savior of the world. It is the perfect opportunity to spread our message far and wide. For the long term, this is what has to be done."

"You're selling out your own people!" Sera shouted.

"I'm advancing an ideology," K'inich said. "Now, please, hand over what's in your satchel. From the second I saw you two enter the holding cell I suspected you might be from the future."

"Is dc Landa a Time Warden, too?" Dak asked.

K'inich looked appalled. "That man could never be part of our movement. He's too blinded by religious zealotry. But he'll make a fine tool." He turned back to Sera. "Now hand over your time-travel device."

"I'll never give it to you," Sera said through her gritted teeth.

K'inich pointed the arrow right at her forehead. "You have three seconds," he said, pulling back on the cocking stirrup.

Riq ripped open Sera's satchel, pulled out the Ring, and set it on the ground in front of her.

"No!" Sera screamed as K'inich reached down to pick it up.

He backed through the doorway, lowering his crossbow. "In case you were wondering," he said, "the neighborhood boy in the story was me. Sometimes destiny finds the man, instead of the man finding his destiny. If the elder who saved my life had been a Hystorian, instead of a Time Warden, who knows? I may have been on your side. But that is not the way events unfolded."

K'inich slammed closed the stone door, and Sera heard the click of the lock.

18

Follow the Snakes

RIQ CURSED himself as he watched Sera pound the stone wall with the undersides of her fists. Why hadn't he trusted his instincts? From the second K'inich had volunteered to accompany them to the observatory, Riq had been skeptical of his motivation. Before that even . . . when he'd asked Sera what she was looking for in the observatory basement. And that story about the two boys in the sea. Riq had sensed all along that something wasn't right. But he had done nothing to stop it. Zero. And now look where they were.

He watched María pacing all around the room with her candle, watched Dak sit against the wall, letting his face fall into his hands. Sera turned around with a panicked look on her face and said, "What now? We'll never get out of here." She looked right at Riq. "Why'd you let him have the Ring?"

"I couldn't let him hurt you," Riq said.

"I'd rather take an arrow in the chest than be stuck in here forever," she said.

"They're probably torching Pacal's codex as we speak," Dak said. "You know, the one we were supposed to protect?"

"I've always known there was an SQ presence here," María said. "But I never once considered Bacab's cousin."

"So, what are we supposed to do?" Sera said. "Sit here and wait for our air to run out? Because that's what'll probably happen."

Dak, Sera, and María continued on like this as Riq began walking around the room, studying every inch of the dark walls. María's candle gave just enough light that he could see. After several minutes he spotted something that made the hairs on his arms stand up. A tiny snake had been carved into one of the stones.

Then another snake, even smaller, on the stone below it.

"And why are *you* so quiet?" Dak shouted at Riq's back. "You don't care that we're all going to die in this tomb?"

Riq ignored Dak and kept scanning farther down the wall. He found a third snake. Then a fourth.

"I know you hear me, Lover Boy!"

"Leave him alone, Dak," Sera said. "Just, please, be quiet for once in your life."

"What did I do to you?" Dak snapped back at her.

María moved in closer to Riq and held her candle to the wall so he could see better. "What are you looking at?" she asked.

"There's a pattern of tiny engravings on the wall," Riq told her. "They go all the way down to the floor."

Sera came to look at them, too. "They're snakes," she said. "Hold on a sec. Dak, get over here with the SQuare."

"Oh, I can't even get a 'please' now?"

Riq turned around, saw Sera take the SQuare from Dak, power it on, and quickly pull up the riddle. "'Dig deep, deeper, deepest,'" she read. She looked up at Riq and Dak and said, "What if this isn't the deepest room in the observatory?"

"Kisa's trying to tell us something," Riq said, scanning stones again. The tiny snake engravings clearly descended all the way down the wall. But the stone closest to the floor had *two* snakes. Maybe that stone was the most significant. He dropped to his knees and began feeling all around the stone. But it felt no different than the others.

"What is it?" Dak asked.

"I don't know yet," Riq told him. He stood up and studied every stone that had a snake on it, starting up near the ceiling. He had to figure this out. What was Kisa trying to tell him? All he saw was a solid stone wall.

"Is there a hidden door or something?" Sera asked.

"What am I not seeing?" Riq mumbled to himself. He felt all around the stones on either side of the ones with snakes. Then he studied the actual engravings. But nothing stood out to him. He grew so frustrated he stood up and punched the wall with a closed fist, which really hurt, so he kicked the stone with two snakes.

A strange thing happened.

The stone he kicked moved a few centimeters into the wall.

Riq turned to look at Dak and Sera, their eyes wide with anticipation.

Riq knelt down and pushed the stone farther and farther into the wall until it revealed a small latch. Riq undid the latch and moved a thick piece of leather to the side to grab the handle underneath. He pulled on it with all his strength. All of the sudden, a small part of the floor came up, revealing a narrow opening that led to a dark staircase.

They all looked at each other, and Sera repeated, "'Deep, deeper, deepest.'"

"This is amazing!" Dak shouted. "I should have been an architect."

The four of them climbed down the narrow stairs, one at a time, Riq now holding María's candle to light the way. When he got to the bottom, he held up the candle and scanned the small room. There was an old wooden desk and a chair. The walls were full of glyphs. The shelves around the desk were covered with rusted lockets and antiquated paintbrushes.

"Oh, wow," Sera said behind him.

"What?" Dak said.

Riq followed Sera's eyes to the floor underneath the desk where there was a full skeleton. His eyes grew big, and he walked over to it and leaned down to get a better look with the candle. There was an open locket near the skeleton's hand. Inside, the glyph for *observatory* was only half finished. He fell to his knees near the skeleton, fighting back tears. He knew in his heart it had to be Kisa.

"Guys!" Dak shouted.

Riq spun around, saw that Dak was holding a codex in his hands.

"Is that what I think it is?" Sera asked.

Riq pulled himself together, got up, and walked over to Dak. He looked at the first panel of the codex. And there it was: the symbol of the ceiba tree. The writing looked slightly different from Pacal's, which told Riq it was a reproduction. He looked up as Sera quoted from the riddle, "'To save the reproduction of the treasure's truth . . .'"

"A copy of Pacal's codex. We found it," Dak said. He took the candle from Riq and circled it all around the room. "Do you know how incredible this is? There probably hasn't been another living soul in this place for hundreds and hundreds of years. At least since she kicked the bucket, right?" He pointed at the skeleton. "I'd assume if anyone found her they'd give her a proper burial."

"I can't believe it," María said. "All along this has been under my feet."

Riq took the candle from Dak and put it in the candleholder on the wall. Now the entire room was dimly lit.

"Um, you guys?" Sera said, pointing at the far wall. "I

just found a glyph etched into a stone near this handle. Can you read it, Riq?"

Riq moved closer to her and read the glyph. "It's an exit," he said.

"Are you kidding me?" Dak started jumping up and down. "There's another way out of here! This Snake Woman was a genius!"

"Easy," Sera warned him. "Let's make sure we can get out before we start patting ourselves on the back. Even then, we still have a lot of work to do switching codices with the monks."

"Come on, Sera," Dak said. "Where's that positive attitude?"

Dak, Sera, and María started trying to turn the handle built into the wall. They barely got it to budge. Sera called out, "Riq, get over here and help us. This thing's rusted in place."

Riq ignored her because he'd just spotted a thin block of wood with a series of painted glyphs. It looked like a letter, placed on the desk for someone to find. Riq picked it up and began reading, his heart now thumping inside his chest.

Dear Future Hystorian,
If you are reading this note it means you have found your way into the birthplace of the Hystorians movement among our people. When I was just a girl, the king of Izamal promised me a secret

room below the basement of his new observatory where I could organize a Hystorian presence. But the king didn't stop there; he built a secret room underneath the secret room. A great many discussions have taken place between these walls. But now I am old, and I fear the end is near. I ask that you help get this message into the hands of the time travelers that may happen to pass through our village a second time.

I initiated the Hystorian presence here because, when I was young, I encountered these three time travelers, and it changed the course of my life. They came during the great storm, and they helped the king maintain possession of our most sacred tool of learning, Pacal's codex. Thousands of young students have been taught from this codex during my lifetime. I can't imagine our village without it.

Riq tried to swallow the lump in his throat. He looked up, saw Dak, Sera, and María all straining to turn the rusted handle. He then looked all around the room and glanced down at the skeleton again. All of it seemed so surreal. Kisa's presence. Her bones beneath the desk. He remembered the young girl he'd sat with at the mouth of the cave. She was so smart and pretty. She made him want to be somebody. And then, in the time it took to snap his fingers, Riq had warped to a different time, and the girl from Izamal had lived an entire life and grown old and died. He turned back to the letter, overwhelmed with emotion.

All my life I'd longed to do something special. When I was young I believed it was art and jewelry. But that changed when I met the time travelers. They arrived with one mission: to save the world. And I realized one day that I could help them by continuing their work. I have been a defender of scholars, and a scholar myself; I have traveled to faraway villages with a message of peace and cooperation; I have warned all Maya to stay vigilant, and to oppose the SQ whenever they might appear on our shores.

The small group of local young people I have trained now refer to me as Akna, after the goddess of motherhood. Even though I never had a child of my own, the name stuck. Most of them went off to other villages to extend our presence. I have done this for over fifty years now. It is my legacy. And I owe my life as a Hystorian to one beautiful young time traveler who walked into my uncle's hut during the great storm.

"Riq, come on!" Sera shouted.

"We got this bad boy open!" Dak shouted. "No thanks to you!"

Riq looked up from the letter, saw Dak, Sera, and María slowly pulling open the door. Behind it he saw yet another set of narrow stone stairs. "One second," he managed to call out to them. And then he turned to the last paragraph of the letter.

Please, Future Hystorian, if you ever happen across these three time travelers, deliver this message to the one named Riq. Tell him my life would never have been what it is if I hadn't spent those three days with him. Tell him he made me believe I could be anything. Tell him he gave me the strength to insist he leave Izamal and continue with his mission, even though I cried for six weeks after with a broken heart. It was the most important decision I ever made, because the world could not be saved without him. And last, Future Hystorian, if this time traveler named Riq ever comes back to Izamal, tell him that Kisa will always remember him, even after I am gone from this earth. Because if it wasn't for our powerful friendship, I never would have fulfilled my destiny as a Hystorian.

"Come on, Riq!" Sera shouted again.

Riq looked up at her, his chest so full it felt like it might burst. The door was open, and Dak and María were already climbing the stairs.

"What's wrong with you?" Sera said. "We have to replace the SQ codex and get back the Ring!"

Riq nodded, set the piece of wood back on the desk, and hurried toward Sera. Before he followed her up the stairs, he took one last look around Kisa's secret room. He remembered seeing her for the first time inside Itchik's hut. That strange feeling in his stomach when their eyes first met. Finally, he understood what it meant.

Riq turned and hurried up the dark stairs, knowing that nothing could stop him now. He was a Hystorian. Just like Kisa was a Hystorian.

And from this point on, he would be as committed to the mission as she had been.

Lover Boy Strikes Back

Dak heaved open the heavy metal hatch, popped his head above the tall grass, and sucked in a deep breath of fresh air. The first thing he saw was smoke billowing into the sky. The monks were already torching everything. Then he noticed the sky itself, which was dull and gray and filled with angry-looking storm clouds.

The secret underground staircase had led to almost the exact spot where they'd warped in: just behind the observatory, in an overgrown patch of wild grass. Dak thought back to when they first arrived and how he'd hardly noticed the grass. Little did he know that it hid a secret passageway that would save their lives. He switched the codex to his left hand and reached down to help María up through the hatch. Then he helped Sera. He stared down into the darkness for a few long seconds, right hand extended, waiting for Riq. But the staircase remained empty.

He turned to Sera. "Where's Lover Boy?"

At that exact moment, Riq came springing up out of the darkness.

Dak noticed the newfound look of determination on the guy's face. Probably because he got to snoop through all of Snake Girl's stuff. He made another mental note about that love seminar he wanted to lead.

"They've already started," Sera said, pointing at the smoke.

"Let's go fix a Break," Dak said, and he took off running toward the square with the codex tucked under his arm like a football. When he glanced back a few seconds into his run, he saw that Sera, Riq, and María were right on his heels.

When they got to the village square, Dak ducked behind a tree to catch his breath and study what was going on. The others sidled up next to him.

There was a massive contained fire burning, its flames shooting twenty feet into the air. Many Mayan people were standing all around the fire, watching their history go up in smoke. Some were holding one another and crying. Others were shouting at the monks. A few were being led away from the square in shackles.

One monk stood at the center of the entire spectacle, waving around a codex as he shouted over the commotion about heaven and hell and the deceitfulness of the devil. Dak couldn't believe the surreal quality of the proceedings. The raging fire and the billowing smoke. De Landa's passionate preaching. The storm clouds hovering ominously over everything, occasionally lit up by a lightning flash.

Back home, Dak had always been drawn to the darker moments of history. He'd climb his favorite tree and read for hours about executions and wars and coups. He could still remember the day he encountered an article about de Landa's *auto-da-fe,* which wiped out at least forty Mayan codices and over twenty thousand cult images. It had amazed him that a monk could be responsible for the torching of an entire civilization's history. But only now did he understand the depth of the man's actions. You just had to look at the faces of the Mayan people watching. It made Dak feel sick to his stomach.

"There they are," Sera said, pointing to the right of the fire. "Bacab and his men. They're coming."

Dak saw them marching toward the village square, a few antiquated weapons cocked and loaded. He understood they'd be no match for the Spanish. Then he spotted K'inich, walking right alongside the brave Mayas, everyone oblivious to the fact that he was using this cultural genocide as an opportunity to advance the SQ agenda.

Dak turned to the others and shouted over the growing commotion, "The monk who's preaching is obviously Diego de Landa."

"And now it will all be burned!" de Landa shouted at the crowd. "And your souls will be cleansed of evil, making it possible for you to see the truth. There is no other way. I will keep only this one document, so future leaders of the church can know what led an entire people to live in darkness!"

"He has no idea he's waving around a fake codex," Sera said.

Dak held up the reproduction of Pacal's codex. "We have to make the switch. Without him knowing, of course. Because he'd never trust us."

"I'll do it," Riq said. "I'm the only one dressed like a monk."

A shot rang out.

Dak spun around, saw one of Bacab's men fall to the ground, holding his chest and choking on his own blood. Another shot was fired. Another man fell.

"They're shooting people!" Sera shouted.

Bacab and the rest of his men scattered, taking cover behind trees and boulders and nearby huts. The scene grew louder with weapons being fired and people yelling and thunder pounding in the sky.

Dak turned back to his friends. "Listen to me!" he shouted. "Riq, same plan as in 638! You hide this one in your robe. I'm going to swipe the one de Landa's holding. You chase me down like you're one of them and we'll switch, okay?"

Riq nodded.

"They'll shoot you, Dak!" Sera cried.

"It's far too dangerous!" María shouted.

Dak looked up when a light rain started to fall. "Kisa did her part," he told them. "Now it's time to do ours." He winked at Riq and moved out from behind the tree.

Thunder crashed overhead as Dak snuck closer to de Landa and the fire. He could already feel the heat seeping into his skin. As soon as de Landa turned his back, still ranting about the devil, Dak darted toward him.

One of the Spaniards shouted at Dak. Another turned and fired an arrow that whistled past Dak's left ear. De Landa turned around just as Dak got to him, but Dak acted quickly, knocking the codex out of his hand, scooping it up, and sprinting away.

Two more arrows whizzed past his head.

Then he heard Riq shouting in Spanish over the commotion, "I've got him! I've got the little thief!"

Riq leapt onto Dak, not only knocking him over but driving his face into the mud near the fire. "You will pay for what you've done!" Riq screamed in his ear, while at the same time slipping Pacal's codex out of his robe. He traded with Dak on the sly, still screaming at him, and then he slugged Dak right in the jaw.

Dak lost his senses for a few seconds, and when he came to he was holding his face and shouting back at Riq in English, "Dude, that wasn't part of the plan!"

But then he looked up and saw three Spaniards aiming arrows at his head.

Riq threw Dak into a tight headlock and ripped Pacal's codex out of his hands. "I have it!" he shouted at the other monks. "Here! Take this back to Brother de Landa! I'll see that this thief pays with his life!"

One of the Spaniards reached for the codex and started toward the preaching man. The other two turned their attention elsewhere.

As Riq aggressively led Dak away, they both snuck glances behind them until they saw that de Landa had possession of Pacal's codex and had resumed his preaching.

"You didn't have to hit me in the jaw," Dak said to Riq.

"It was the only way," Riq told him. And then he glanced down at Dak, grinning slightly, and added, "Oh, and I'd prefer you didn't refer to me as 'Lover Boy.'"

Dak rolled his eyes, then ordered Riq to guide him closer to the fire so he could torch the SQ codex. "No one will ever read these lies again," he said.

They only made it a few steps closer, though, before getting bowled over. Dak pulled his face from the mud again and looked up. It was K'inich, who shouted, "I saw what you just did!"

The SQ codex had fallen out of Riq's robe, into the mud, and the three of them wrestled for it. "Give it to me!" K'inich shouted. "Now!" He punched Riq in the side of the face and reached for the loose codex, but Dak was too quick. He pounced on it, clutching it to his chest and curling his body into a ball. K'inich slugged him in the kidneys and the back of his head, and then Riq wrestled K'inich's arms behind his back.

The rain fell harder.

Thunder exploded directly over their heads.

Dak squeezed the codex to his chest as Riq and K'inich fell on top of him, ripping and clawing at each other's faces.

A monk suddenly hurried over with a raised gun, shouting, "Stop! Stop! Get off him!"

Dak relaxed some, assuming the monk was ordering K'inich to get off Riq, but when he looked up, he saw the monk cracking Riq in the back of the head with the butt of his gun.

K'inich scurried to his feet and handed over the Infinity Ring, shouting at the monk, "Throw it into the fire! I'll take care of the codex!" He took the gun from the monk and stuck it into Dak's ear, shouting, "That's right! The SQ has men on *both* sides!" He shackled Dak's and Riq's wrists and began pushing them away from the square.

As they were led away, Dak turned and watched the monk hurrying toward the fire with the Ring.

"Sera!" Dak shouted.

She was beside Bacab now, who was aiming his crossbow at de Landa. He fired an arrow that narrowly missed. Two monks converged on de Landa immediately, pushing his head down and leading him toward a nearby hut. Dak saw that de Landa was still clutching Pacal's codex.

Lightning lit up the massive storm clouds.

Thunder pounded so forcefully it shook the earth under Dak's feet.

Everywhere he looked Spaniards were shackling Mayas. The fire roared, all of Izamal's history quickly turning to ash. He spotted the monk still marching the Ring toward the flames.

"Sera!" Dak shouted again.

K'inich stopped leading him and Riq away long enough to bash the gun against the side of Dak's head. "Quiet!" he shouted. "I don't know how you got out, but I will now get rid of you once and for all! No one can stop our mission!"

Sera screamed.

Dak looked up, saw that she had leapt onto the back of the SQ monk who had the Infinity Ring. He elbowed her off and kicked her in the gut.

"No!" Dak shouted.

K'inich smashed him in the ear again. Dak shuddered in pain. He opened his eyes in time to see the monk wind up and heave the Ring all the way into the middle of the raging fire.

Bacab threw down his crossbow and sprinted right into the fire to retrieve it. He disappeared for several seconds, then came racing back out, his hair and clothes in flames, and tossed the Ring to safety. He then dove into the mud and rolled around until the flames were extinguished. He hopped back up, badly burned, and picked up the Ring.

"Watch out!" Sera screamed from the ground.

A Spaniard had stepped out from behind a large boulder, aiming a crossbow right at Bacab. He fired, the arrow burrowing into Bacab's back.

Bacab dropped to his knees, arching his back and reaching a hand behind himself, trying to touch the arrow.

"Bacab!" Sera shouted, struggling to her feet.

The monk reloaded and fired a second arrow, this one sinking into Bacab's right thigh.

Dak watched another Mayan man finally pounce on the monk, ripping the crossbow out of his hands. And he watched Sera sprint to Bacab, helping him to his feet, throwing his arm around her shoulder. She started half-carrying him out of the chaotic scene.

More lightning flashed.

Dak was entirely helpless.

K'inich pulled him and Riq behind a hut, and threw them on the ground. He raised the gun at them, shouting, "Now you will die!"

Dak squeezed closed his eyes and waited for the sound of the shot that would end his life.

He heard a crashing sound instead, and when he

looked up, he saw María standing over K'inich's motionless body, holding a large, jagged rock in her hands. Her eyes were full of tears as she looked at Dak and Riq and said, "I will never let Akna's work be in vain."

Dak glanced at Riq, then watched María take the gun and keys off K'inich and hurry over to unlock the shackles. She tried several keys before finally inserting the right one and freeing them. Dak flexed his hands for a few seconds, then ripped the SQ codex out of K'inich's limp hands and raced out from behind the hut, toward the fire.

It was smaller now because the rain was stronger, but Dak knew it would burn the SQ's lies just the same. As he flung the thing deep into the flames, he slipped in the wet mud. He watched from his knees as the fake codex caught fire. Some of the pages twisted under the intense heat, then shriveled up into brittle red and black sheets, the embers eventually breaking off and lifting up into the stormy sky.

Now the world would never know the lies and propaganda of the SQ's codex. They'd learn the truth about the Maya instead. Some of it.

Dak breathed heavily as he continued watching the fire.

More thunder pounded overhead and the skies opened up.

Rain poured down on Dak's head, flooding the ground around him, forcing the few remaining monks to cower and run for shelter. But Dak couldn't take his eyes off the fire. Yes, they'd fixed the Break, but they'd failed to stop de Landa's *auto-de-fe*. And Dak was overwhelmed by how much had been lost today. He realized what a vile and violent act it was to destroy a culture's history. It was almost like murder.

Lightning lit up the dark storm clouds again.

Thunder roared.

Dak sensed someone hovering over him, and when he looked up, he found a drenched Riq standing there, holding out his hand to Dak.

2 0

Beneath the Ceiba Tree

"PLEASE, JUST talk to me," Bacab said to Sera.

Tears were falling down her cheeks, but she didn't care. Bacab was badly hurt. He said he knew he wouldn't make it and refused to let her take him to the village medicine man.

"Talk about what?" Sera asked, wiping her face with the back of her hand.

"It does not matter, little sister. Tell me about your life. Your family."

Sera watched the way his entire body shivered in the warm, humid air. She looked out from behind the large ceiba tree they had ducked beneath, trying to figure out what she could tell a dying man. Rain poured down all around them. Large drops sometimes slipped through the thick tree leaves and landed on their heads. She had tried the door to the hut in front of them, but it was locked. And nobody had answered when she knocked, even though she was sure there were people inside.

"Please," he said, closing his eyes and leaning his head against the trunk of the tree. "Anything."

Sera squeezed Bacab's cold hand until he opened his eyes again. "It's only me and my uncle Diego," she said.

"No parents?" Bacab asked in a strained voice.

Sera shook her head. "I never knew them."

The wind picked up, swirling around Sera and Bacab and their tree. The leaves rustled wildly. Sera heard a thick branch snap, but when she looked up she didn't see anything.

"Tell me more," Bacab said.

"I had a dream about them," she said, wiping mud from Bacab's brow. "My parents. I was in the future. Thousands of years from now, when the world was ending. I went to my uncle's barn and opened the door. And there they were, sitting in chairs, waiting for me."

"That's right," Bacab said.

Sera wiped the tears from her face again and said, "They came back because they cared about me."

"Of course they did." Bacab coughed and reached down to touch the arrow in his thigh. "You will see them again."

Sera let out a sob and then quickly stopped herself. "I'm sorry, Bacab. This was all my fault. You were trying to help me."

"Since I was a little boy," he said in almost a whisper, "I wanted to be a leader of people. *My* people."

He coughed and wiped his mouth. "My father always warned me, though. He said, 'Bacab, if you want to be someone special you must have strong shoulders.' I didn't understand until now."

Sera's heart was pounding in her chest. It was exactly what her grandfather had said to her. The one time they'd met. She stared at Bacab, trying to swallow the lump in her throat.

The sky lit up in a massive flash of lightning.

Thunder rumbled directly overhead.

"What about you, little sister?" Bacab asked. "Do you have strong shoulders?"

Sera sobbed again, and this time when she tried to catch herself, she wasn't able to. She just kept on crying.

"I think you do," he said, grinning a little. "And I sense things." He coughed hard and then pulled in a deep breath. "About people."

Tears streamed down Sera's face, and she tried for a deep breath, too. But she couldn't get one. She was too upset. "Bacab," she said. She wanted to say something important, something meaningful and comforting. But the words weren't coming into her head and all she could think to do was say his name again. "Bacab."

When he didn't answer, she let herself sob into her own hands.

Because she knew.

He was gone.

After several seconds she leaned his head back against

the trunk of the ceiba tree and pushed closed his eyelids. "I'm proud to come from you," she whispered.

Then she leaned her head against the tree, too, and watched the growing storm.

A few minutes later, Dak and Riq were there. Dak gripped the Infinity Ring in his hands. Riq was fiddling with his bracelet.

Sera looked up at them, both soaking wet. She wiped her face and climbed to her feet.

"Sera," Dak started. But then he noticed Bacab and said, "Oh."

Riq gently patted her on the shoulder. "Some of the villagers have warned us that the storm will be getting much worse," he said. "But we can stay here a little longer if you want."

"It's a storm," Dak said. "But I don't think it's going to be as bad as they were saying."

Sera took the Infinity Ring from Dak and programmed in the new coordinates Riq showed her on the SQuare. She looked up at Dak and Riq and said, "If the Maya say a great storm is coming, then a great storm is coming."

They nodded.

"Better hold on if you're coming with me," she said.

Dak and Riq both put their hands on the Ring next to hers, and she pushed the button that would send them warping through time yet again. The Ring began to vibrate, and the liquid inside lit up and swirled. Sera looked out at the blurring Mayan landscape, feeling sad but also incredibly full. She turned to look at Bacab, thinking how the next time someone in school drew her great-great-great-grandmother sitting on a Mayan temple, she would not feel embarrassed. She would feel proud.

Everything around them began to blur. Dak said to Riq, "Show her."

Riq held up an open locket. Sera expected to see a Mayan glyph in the last second before they warped away. But it was something else altogether.

"Is that . . . Chinese?" she asked.

Just as Dak opened his mouth to answer, they were whisked away into blackness.